RONSDALE PRESS
3350 West 21st Avenue, Vancouver, B.C., Canada V6S 1G7
www.ronsdalepress.com

Typesetting: Julie Cochrane, in Minion 12 pt on 16
Cover Art & Design: Nancy de Brouwer Alofli Graphic Design
Paper: Ancient Forest Friendly "Silva" — 100% post-consumer waste,
    totally chlorine-free and acid-free

Ronsdale Press wishes to thank the Canada Council for the Arts, the Govern-
ment of Canada through the Book Publishing Industry Development Program
(BPIDP), and the Province of British Columbia through the British Columbia
Arts Council for their support of its publishing program.

Library and Archives Canada Cataloguing in Publication

Roy, Philip, 1960–
    Submarine outlaw / Philip Roy.

ISBN 978-1-55380-058-3

I. Title.

PS8635.O91144S83 2008   jC813'.6   C2008-900529-5

At Ronsdale Press we are committed to protecting the environment. To this end
we are working with Markets Initiative (www.oldgrowthfree.com) and printers
to phase out our use of paper produced from ancient forests. This book is one
step towards that goal.

Printed in Canada by Marquis Printing, Quebec

for Thomas

ACKNOWLEDGEMENTS

The author would like to thank Ronald Hatch for his direction and diligence and Veronica Hatch for choosing Alfred in the first place. Many thanks also to the Writers Federation of Nova Scotia, where dedicated people are gathered to help aspiring writers. Thanks to Jane Buss, who is a beacon in the Canadian writing community. And thanks in particular to my mother, Ellen Roy, for her unfailing love and support.

Chapter One

I never dreamed of being an outlaw.

Growing up in Dark Cove, a tiny fishing village in northern Newfoundland, I dreamed of far away places and exciting adventures. My grandfather thought differently. He told me I'd be a fisherman when I grew up, just like everybody else.

"What do you do exactly?" I asked.

"Well . . . we get up early," he said. "That's the first thing. And we have fish for breakfast. That's always a good idea. Then we go down to the wharf and start the motors and check the oil and discuss the weather and decide where to fish that day."

"And then?"

"And then we go out and fish."

"How long do you fish?"

"All day. Then we come back, put the fish in the ice house, hang up the nets, clean up the boats and go home."

"And then?"

"Then we have supper. Usually fish. Sometimes fish cakes. Once in a while your grandmother makes a great fish stew."

"Then what do you do?"

"We sit around the kitchen and talk about the day."

"Like what?"

"Oh . . . the weather, the sea, how many fish we caught that day."

"And the next day?"

"The next day's the same."

"And the next?"

"The same. It's pretty much always the same. You'll see soon enough. Don't worry, you'll make a good fisherman. It's in your blood."

All night I tossed and turned. In the morning I went to see my grandfather.

"I don't want to be a fisherman," I said.

"What? Of course you do. It's in your blood."

"I don't think it's in my blood. I can't feel it."

My grandfather laughed.

"It's not something you can feel. It just is."

"But I feel something else in my blood."

"Do you now? What's that?"

"I think I am an explorer."

"An *explorer*?"

"Yes."

"Gee, I think everything is pretty much explored already."

"Really?"

"I think so."

"The whole world?"

"Yup, I think so. Except maybe the ocean."

I went down to the beach and skipped some rocks and stared at the ocean. It didn't make sense to be an explorer if everything had already been explored. But surely there were jungles never seen before. And deserts. Surely there were mountains no one had climbed and plains no one had crossed and islands no one had set foot upon.

Surely there were creatures no one had ever seen — like three-legged beasts and seven-legged bugs. After all, if a snake had one leg, a monkey two, a dog four, a starfish five, a ladybug six and an octopus eight, why wouldn't there be creatures with three and seven legs? I mean, there were birds that swam under water, fish that flew, pigs that lived underground and frogs that lived in trees. Who could say that everything had been discovered? Besides, my grandfather was only a fisherman, not an explorer. Perhaps only an explorer could believe in things not yet found.

I climbed the hill, crossed the woods and passed the junkyard. It was owned by Ziegfried, an angry man, twice the size of the biggest fisherman. It was said he was so mean he couldn't even keep a junkyard dog — they were too afraid of him. I always wondered how he stayed in business if he was so mean. But the junkyard was a treasure-hunter's paradise. I could stare at it through a hole in the fence for hours.

I wandered over to the fence to take a peek. There, in the midst of piles of junk, I saw something that would change my life. I couldn't see the whole of it, just one corner, but it was round, smooth, black and beautiful. A submarine! A small one. I twisted my head to get a better look. I moved to another crack in the fence but it wasn't any better. In desperation I pulled the board back and forth, until it came away from the fence altogether. Now I could see, but there were still piles of junk in the way. I poked my head through and looked around. It was dead silent. Not a soul in sight. I squeezed through the fence and crept across the junkyard towards the submarine.

"Halt!" boomed a voice. "Or I'll blow you to smithereens!"

I froze.

"Please don't shoot me!"

I turned my head just enough to see that the gun Ziegfried was holding was actually a broom.

"What the heck are you doing?" he yelled. "This is private property. Get out quick or I'll blow you to smithereens!"

"I'm sorry," I said. "I just wanted to take a closer look at the submarine."

"Submarine? What submarine? There's no submarine here, boy. You must be dreaming. Now, hit the road!"

I started towards the fence. Turning, I pointed to the submarine.

"*That* submarine."

He looked over.

"What? That? That's no submarine. That's just an old oil tank. Boy, you've got some imagination. Hah!"

I stared at the tank. It had looked so much like a submarine. I climbed out through the fence, but my imagination got the better of me and I stuck my head back in.

"What would it take to turn it into a submarine?"

"What? Turn that old tank into a submarine?"

Ziegfried made the strangest face. His brow tightened, his eyes narrowed and his mouth twisted to one side as his brain went to work. He began to list off things it would take.

"Well . . . a motor, for starters. Maybe a light diesel engine."

"Like a boat engine?"

"No . . . too noisy and heavy. A submarine has to be quiet."

I nodded, though I really had no idea.

"Then . . . a keel, rudder, stabilizing fins, portal, propeller. Ai yi yi."

He rubbed his forehead.

"Let's see . . . batteries, sonar system, depth gauges, insulation, air compressors, sleeping quarters, heating, air-conditioning. Heavens . . . !"

He stared at the tank feverishly while his mind continued to count what was needed.

I stepped back in.

"How long would it take?"

"What?"

The question broke his concentration, and he had to start all over again.

"Oh. Let's see . . ."

There was a long pause. And then, "Three years. Maybe four."

"Three years!"

My heart sank. I would be fifteen then. It seemed like a lifetime. Who could wait so long?

"Or longer," he said. "It depends."

"On what?"

"On many things."

I suddenly realized how foolish I had been. I had thought an old tank was a submarine, or could become one in just a few months. It was the first time I realized I had been completely unrealistic. Nothing had ever made me feel so much like a child before. Now I had to wonder about my other beliefs. Were they unrealistic too? Should I just accept becoming a fisherman like my grandfather? Before I could think about it too much, Ziegfried said something wonderful.

"Well . . . I need to put some things down on paper. You'd better come back tomorrow."

"Come back tomorrow?"

He nodded and walked away, deep in thought.

I couldn't believe it. I climbed back through the fence. Suddenly something occurred to me. I stuck my head inside again.

"My name is Alfred."

"Ziegfried."

"I can't pay you anything," I yelled.

Without turning around, he yelled back, "I can't pay you anything either."

Chapter Two

The next day I walked through the front entrance, past the "Beware Guard Dogs" sign. I knew there were no dogs. Besides, I had been invited; there was no reason to be afraid. And yet, I was a little. Ziegfried was such a large man with such a ferocious temper. At least that's what people said.

There was a plain house in the front. The junkyard had grown up around it. I came to the door and knocked. When Ziegfried opened the door I saw and heard birds, dozens of them, squawking and chirping and jumping around in their cages like monkeys. Ziegfried didn't keep junkyard dogs; he kept junkyard birds.

He stood in the doorway with a puzzled look, as if he had completely forgotten why I was there. Instead of saying hello, he just blurted out, "A Beetle!"

"A Beetle?" I said. "What's that?"

"An engine."

He grabbed his coat and started across the junkyard without waiting for me to follow.

"A Volkswagen engine," said Ziegfried. "That's what we want. It's small, efficient and easy to repair. I have lots of them."

I caught up and walked beside him. I could feel my heart pounding in my chest. We passed the oil tank and I noticed he had cleared junk away. At the far end was a row of Volkswagens, some on top of others. Some had no windshields or tires. Ziegfried went to the back of one.

"Isn't the engine in the front?"

He looked at me strangely.

"Not in a Beetle."

He lifted the back hood.

"It's a tight little engine. If we pack insulation around it we can quiet it down some. But we need batteries, and another backup, for emergencies. Do you ride a bicycle?"

"Yes."

"Good. We can rig a bicycle gear to the drive shaft . . . in case the engine breaks down or you run out of gas."

"Oh. Is that a lot of work?"

He turned and looked right into my eyes. For the first time I saw that he was really a very different person from

what his voice and size suggested. Beneath his bushy eyebrows his eyes were soft and tender.

"*Everything* is a lot of work. But what else are we here for,
eh, if not to work?"

He made a sweeping gesture over the junkyard.

"What is the point of all of this, eh, if we don't put it to
work?"

"I guess so."

"Good then. We will begin by pulling the engine out of
this Beetle. Okay?"

"Okay!"

So we rolled a tripod to the Beetle and Ziegfried showed
me how to disconnect the motor and hoist it into the air
and swing it onto a trolley. We pushed the trolley across the
yard into a shed and hoisted the motor onto a workbench.

"Good. Now we take apart everything that comes apart,
clean it and put it back together. Got it?"

"Got it."

I learned more about engines that day than I thought I
ever would in a lifetime. But as interesting as the engine was
itself, and all the tools we used, the most fascinating thing
was watching Ziegfried work. In our village all the people
worked with their hands, one way or another, but I had
never seen anyone work like this. It was as if his hands were
performing a ballet. They never moved quickly and never
lingered in one place but were always in motion — smooth,
steady and confident — like dancers on a stage. And they

continued dancing even when his head was occupied else-where, as if they had a mind of their own. Ziegfried said there was nothing so smooth as a clean, well-greased motor, but I didn't think any motor could ever match the rhythmi-cal precision of his hands at work.

After several hours that flew by like minutes, he said it was time to feed his friends. I knew he meant the birds.

"Can you come back tomorrow?"

I nodded.

"This is my summer vacation. I can come every day."

"Good. There is a *lot* of work to do."

He turned to a sink, splashed green soap over his hands, washed them and went into his house. He never said good-bye and never looked back. I watched him go. Then I went to the sink and did exactly the same. I walked out through the gate and headed home. I was so happy I thought I could fly.

Over the summer we replaced parts in the motor and got it running so smoothly it was almost singing. We cut holes in the tank for the portal, air and water valves, drive shaft and observation window. Ziegfried cut the holes with a welding torch and I filed the edges smooth. It really *was* a lot of work. My arms and shoulders ached terribly and I noticed muscles developing on my arms and belly. My appetite doubled, then tripled.

Once the holes were cut I climbed inside with a flash-light. It was filthy. I felt discouraged. I couldn't imagine it

ever being clean enough to ride in. Ziegfried laughed and assured me it would be.

"Don't worry. Once we scrub her out and line her with cedar she'll smell like a lady in church. You'll see. But that's a ways off yet. There's a lot of ground to cover first."

Was there ever! In fact, the work was really endless. But it was usually interesting. I was always learning new things and getting stronger. I was often on my own, rooting through piles of scrap for a gear or a flywheel or any number of bolts. But sometimes we worked at the same table and the work was quiet and we could talk. Those were my favourite times. Then I could ask questions. And sometimes he would.

"So, what do your parents think of your coming here every day?"

"I live with my grandparents. My mother died when I was born. I never knew her."

"And your father?"

"He left when my mother died. I guess he didn't want to be a fisherman either."

"You don't want to be a fisherman?"

"No. I want to be an explorer."

"Good for you! There are too many fishermen and not enough explorers!"

One day I asked Ziegfried if *he* had ever been a fisherman.

"Heavens no! I've got a mortal fear of the sea. I don't care

how I die; I just don't want to drown. How about you? I presume if you're going to ride around in a submarine you're not afraid of the water?"

"I love the ocean, and I'm not afraid of drowning."

"Good thing. You know, it would be a good idea to practise diving the way pearl fishers do, and build up your lung capacity. They hold onto stones that pull them down quickly, and let go when they're deep enough. It could save your life in an emergency. Do you think you could do that?"

"I'd love to do that!"

"Good. I'd go with you but . . ."

"I'm already used to diving for shells and coins and stuff."

"Perfect! We can rig a line with markers every five feet to tell you where you are. Then you can practise until you're an expert. By the time the submarine is ready you'll be a fish."

So we went through the junkyard and found a spool of cable a hundred feet long.

"It's plenty. If you can dive half this deep, you're doing pretty good."

At home I asked my grandfather how deep the water was at the wharf.

"Oh, it must be pretty near thirty feet in places. Gets deeper as you go out. Why do you ask?"

"I'm just curious. How far out do you have to go to reach fifty feet?"

"Fifty feet? Oh, you'll probably hit fifty feet a quarter of

a mile out, except for Deep Cove. Deep Cove's got a drop-off about a hundred feet or so right off the beach. I know that because there's an old schooner down there and we thought maybe we could raise her once. That was a long time ago. We dropped a cable a good hundred feet before we hit bottom. But she was too heavy. We burnt out the motor of the hoist and snapped the cable before we even moved her. I don't think anybody's tried since."

"Oh. Thanks."

"Listen now: you be careful if you ever go in the water around Deep Cove 'cause there's an undertow. A young fellah I used to know drowned there fifty years ago. An undertow is an unpredictable thing. It's not there one minute and the next it is."

I nodded.

"I'm always careful."

"You swim like a fish, don't you? I've never known a fisherman who could swim."

"I don't plan on being a fisherman."

"So you say. You've got lots of time to change your mind."

"I won't change my mind."

"We'll see."

"I won't change my mind."

Chapter Three

At Deep Cove I started preparing to dive. It was important to be careful with everything, and I was. I gathered logs and tied them together to make a raft. I wrapped a rope around one log and buried it in the sand and tied the other end to the raft so it wouldn't float away. Then I piled stones on the raft and paddled out past the drop off. I lowered the cable into the water and watched the markers disappear. Down they went in a straight line, which meant there wasn't any undertow. Ziegfried said that pearl divers took deep breaths first, so I closed my eyes and breathed deeply. Then I opened them, picked up a stone and jumped off the raft.

It pulled me down pretty fast. There was the five-foot-marker, the ten, then the fifteen. It seemed to take a long time to reach the twenty, and suddenly there was pressure in my ears. I passed the twenty-five-foot marker but my ears were starting to hurt and it was beginning to get dark. The thirty-foot-marker was approaching but something — I didn't know what exactly — made me uncomfortable and I let go. Then I was glad because the swim back up took a lot longer than coming down.

On the raft again, it all seemed very different.

"I can do better than that."

Resting for a few moments, I picked up another stone, took a couple of deep breaths and jumped off again. Down I went through a column of bubbles. In no time there was the fifteen-foot marker, the twenty, the twenty-five. But my ears hurt again and I let go. Once again, swimming up took a lot longer than sinking with the stone. The surface of the water spread out like a sheet of silver above me. But it was disappointing. I'd never make much of an explorer if I couldn't try harder than that. Ziegfried said that pearl divers also slowed their heartbeats. Picking up another stone, I closed my eyes and tried to relax. A calm came over me. I slipped off the raft more gently and went down with the stone. At twenty-five feet my ears started to hurt but I ignored them and held on for the thirty-foot marker.

"That's better," I thought as I swam up to the surface.

But it was further to go and I was out of breath at the top.

After five more dives it was enough for one day. The deepest I had been able to reach was thirty feet.

"Thirty feet!" said Ziegfried. "That's terrific! Gee! Was the water cold?"

"A little."

"Was it dark?"

"Not really. It started to get dark. I couldn't see the bottom."

"Ai yi yi. You're a braver man than I am, Al."

I beamed. I didn't usually like to be called Al, but the way Ziegfried said it was okay.

"Well, you better get in as much diving as you can because the fall's almost here and the water will soon be too cold."

I nodded.

"What will we do in the winter, when it's too cold to work outside?"

"Work inside."

I looked around.

"Where?"

"We'll build a shelter around the sub. Posts and plastic. Two layers. Heat it with hot air. I've got half a dozen generators. We'll put the whole thing together in a day."

It took less than a day. We dug holes for the posts and supported them with concrete blocks. We cut heavy-duty plastic sheets from a large roll and made a two-layered wall

with five inches between, through which we blew hot air from a gas generator. With another generator we heated the inside of the makeshift shed. In the afternoon, just as we finished, it started to rain. It rained for the next two weeks straight. I always wondered how he had known exactly when to enclose the sub.

Diving *did* get a lot colder. I braved it until the middle of October before calling it quits. I carried a jacket out to the raft and put it on between each dive. That helped. Still, I shivered and my skin turned blue. On one dive I reached forty feet, without much ear pain. That was encouraging. But the sky was dark and so was the sea. At forty feet I couldn't see more than ten or fifteen feet away. At one moment I had the feeling there was something there, like a large fish, or seal, close by and watching me. It was spooky but I didn't panic.

"You've got nerves of steel!" Ziegfried said later.

Then he looked very serious.

"Well, I suppose what you're planning to do will require nothing less. Do you think about that, Al? Do you think of the danger of it all, the risks you'll be taking — sitting in a tiny sub, surrounded by freezing water, hundreds, maybe thousands of miles from any land?"

"I think I am an explorer," I said, speaking from my heart. "I think sometimes I *will* be afraid but I am willing to accept that. I think that all explorers know there are risks

and dangers, but they are driven on anyway. That's how I feel."

"Well, I take my hat off to you. It makes me proud to work on the ship of a real explorer. Now, let's get back to work."

Oh, the endless work! There was work people loved and work people hated and work that simply had to be done. My grandfather loved fishing, but I would have hated it. Ziegfried loved fiddling with machines and inventing things but didn't care to go exploring. He said that when people loved their work, it was hardly work at all. That's how I felt about exploring, even though I hadn't done it yet. I just knew. I didn't love cleaning and preparing equipment for the submarine, but it was work that had to be done and so I did it. What drove me on was the thought of where it would take me one day.

Over the fall and winter I came to the junkyard every afternoon and weekend. I told my grandparents that Ziegfried was helping me build a submarine in exchange for helping out in the yard. This was more or less true. No doubt they didn't take the submarine seriously, but they didn't stop me from going either. Likely they were happy I had found a way to keep busy.

One day there might be no customers; the next, we'd be continually interrupted by people looking for hubcaps, metal fencing, sinks, toilets, bathtubs and so on. Sometimes

people brought in things to sell. Watching Ziegfried buy and sell helped me better understand why people thought he was so mean and scary. But it was just an act. If they knew what he was really like, they would probably have taken advantage of him. When someone brought something in, he would frown and say the item was pretty much worthless. Only at the last minute would he offer a meager price, which was usually accepted. On the other hand, when someone wanted to buy something, Ziegfried exaggerated its value and seemed unwilling to part with it, agreeing only at the last minute if the customer had clearly reached his highest offer. And he always wore an angry face. I had to turn around so the customer wouldn't see me grinning. This — the buying and selling — was work Ziegfried hated, but had to do if he wanted to stay in business.

One day my grandfather insisted on giving me a ride to the junkyard, obviously to check out the situation. I introduced him to Ziegfried. My grandfather looked up at the towering junk dealer, who stared back, and the two men shook hands without saying a word. I couldn't take my eyes off their hands when they clasped. Though my grandfather was a much smaller man, his hands were larger. His knuckles protruded like the knots in a tree. To me it looked as if the sea were shaking hands with the land.

In the winter was welding, welding and more welding, which meant endless filing. Ziegfried would say, "Now, we weld the portal."

That meant that *he* would weld the portal and I would file it smooth. There was also the drilling of holes and riveting. The tank had to be reinforced inside and out. Ziegfried's plan was to build an interior of wood, both to insulate and strengthen the sub. He sketched diagrams with beams ingeniously crisscrossing the inside.

I stared at the diagrams.

"But . . . won't I bang my head?"

He bent over the diagrams and stared closely.

"No. You will duck."

We got the tank cleaned out and put a heater inside until the metal was bone dry. Ziegfried took endless measurements and made calculations for the position of everything. He measured my height, width and weight, allowing for growth. Then he designed the interior around me.

It was a one-man sub. There would be one seat at the controls, one stationary bicycle, one bed and only enough space for one person to move around comfortably. After the wood interior was installed I could expect to stand up straight, with four inches to spare. If I grew more than four inches I would have to bend my head. If I stood with my arms outstretched I could almost touch both sides. The stern would house several waterproof compartments and storage, and the bow would feature an observation window in the floor. The bicycle would be placed in the very center, to allow the greatest freedom of movement for pedalling, and for stability.

The engine would be installed in the stern and encased

in its own separate compartment, lined with insulation. A steel wall, with door, would be constructed to separate the engine compartment, air-compressors, batteries, hydraulic and electrical systems, from the rest of the sub, which would enable me to shut myself off in case of fire or flooding in those areas. Ziegfried was working on an automatic system for pumping water out of each area of the sub. His idea was to have several sump pumps — each with its own battery source — which would automatically engage whenever water started filling the room or compartment. The air inside the sub would come from pressurized tanks, which would regulate automatically. New air would come from the tanks, which I would periodically refill on the surface; old air would jettison through a valve.

On the outside he welded two tanks on opposite sides of the sub, which would serve as ballast. Part of each tank would be permanently filled with air to allow for minimum buoyancy; otherwise, I lived with the risk of the sub plunging to the ocean floor. Two hundred feet was as far as he felt the sub should go, which didn't seem very deep to me, considering the ocean stretched down five miles in places.

"Oh, you might dive three or four hundred feet," said Ziegfried. "But by five hundred you'll be popping rivets and inviting the ocean into your lap. Go down a mile or so and the pressure will flatten the sub like a sheet of paper."

The function of the ballast tanks was fairly simple: if you wanted to dive, you let water in. If you wanted to rise, you

blew water out by forcing air into the tanks from the compressors. Ziegfried was also working on a design for a manual inflation of the tanks.

"Murphy's Law," he said. "If something can go wrong, it *will*. We have to have back-up systems to our back-up systems. You can never be too safe in a submarine."

Spring came and the submarine began to look like a *real* submarine. We kept it enclosed in its plastic shed to keep curious customers from poking around and gossiping. We dragged junk over and placed it around the shed to make it look like a long-abandoned project. Finally, it was time to begin the wood interior. I thought that meant we were getting close to finishing. The hope started to grow in me that somehow the sub might be seaworthy before the next winter. I could hardly contain it. One day it slipped out.

"Do you think I could try out the sub by the end of summer?"

"Heavens above! We've got to cut the wood, steam it, bend it, fit it, sand it and stain it. *Then* we can start on the systems. We've got the engine and drive shaft to install; the pumps, air system, hydraulic, electrical, safety, communications, navigation . . ."

He dropped his arms, took a long stare at me and sighed. I got such a knot in my stomach I had to sit down. We had been working so hard. Suddenly I saw the childishness of my impatience. I realized what an insult it was to his dedication

and workmanship. How I wished I could take the question back. Never again would I make such a childish outburst again.

"It was a stupid thing to ask," I said quietly as we resumed our work.

"Aye!" said Ziegfried, with a smile, "It was the stupidest thing I've heard in years."

Chapter Four

I counted the days until school ended and I was free for the summer. It coincided with two other important events: the ocean had warmed enough for diving again, and I turned thirteen.

"One more year," said my grandfather, "and you'll come out on the fishing boat. I started fishing when I was four-teen and so did my father."

It didn't seem to matter to my grandfather that most kids in Canada stayed in school until they were seventeen or eighteen. You didn't need an education to fish, he said. You had to read and write; everything else you could learn on

the boat. After that, I told myself the submarine *had* to be ready by the time I turned fourteen. If it weren't, I would stay in the woods until it was.

The ocean had warmed enough for diving but you couldn't exactly call it warm. Once again, I wore a jacket between dives. And I shivered and my skin turned blue. The raft had to be rebuilt. The winter had ripped it apart and strewn its logs across the beach. But I reached forty feet on my first dive and felt pretty good. At forty feet I thought I saw the outline of the ship. It was kind of eerie. Before I went home I managed to touch the forty-five-foot marker. At forty-five feet I was pretty sure what was below was the old schooner.

"Well, that was before I came here," said Ziegfried afterwards. "But I have heard about it. What I wouldn't give to raise her and see what's salvageable. But Alfred, forty-five feet! Now, that's something to be proud of."

"Well, I *am* a year older."

"And a year wiser. In many ways."

I smiled. A compliment from Ziegfried really meant something; he did not waste words.

The summer rolled along at a sluggish pace, which suited me fine. I hoped we would get more done than expected. But Ziegfried would never rush the work. Working with wood did not come as natural to him as metal. He would speak of the "virtues" of an engine, or the "strengths" of metal, but he always referred to the "difficulties" of wood.

Metal was obedient, he said; wood had a mind of its own. This was particularly true in the tedious job of steaming and bending the wood. We cut narrow strips of cedar, maple and pine, steamed them until they were soft and pliable, then stretched them over a frame corresponding to the shape they would take inside the sub. For every three or four strips that molded into the shape we wanted, there was always one that twisted up like a fiddlehead. I saw the frustration on Ziegfried's face grow.

"Oh, go your own way then!" he would say to the twisted piece of wood. "We don't want you anyway."

The wood had come piecemeal over the winter and spring. He traded for it whenever possible. I thought we had more than enough, but once it was cut to shape and the scrap discarded there was never enough. We were always on the lookout for more cedar, especially. It was best suited to water, Ziegfried said.

Once we started to fit the wood into place, the interior began to resemble something vaguely habitable. Next to the touch of metal, the wood was soft and warm and pleasing to the eye. I got a wave of excitement every time I came into the shed and saw what we had accomplished the day before.

Then one morning Ziegfried was sitting on his back step, dressed in a black suit and wearing a mournful look on his face. He held a suitcase by his side. I was bewildered.

"I've got to ask you a favour, Al."

"Of course. Anything."

"It's my poor old mother. Her time has come and I've got to go and see her. I'll be gone for a week. Can you keep the yard for me and feed my friends?"

"Of course. I'll look after everything. Don't worry about a thing."

"I left instructions for their feeding. Give everybody fresh water twice a day. And don't put your fingers in the Kaiser's cage, or you might lose them."

"Which one is the Kaiser?"

"The biggest one. He's friendly enough once he gets to know you, but watch your fingers."

"Okay. I hope your mother's okay."

He sighed, got up and walked towards the gate. He never looked back; just raised his hand. Then he was gone.

I went to the shed, looked in and thought of things to do. There was wood to sand and tools to sharpen. Ziegfried said that working with dull tools was like drinking from a cup with a hole in the bottom. I could do those things, and clean up. Instead, I stepped out of the shed and stared at the yard. Oddly, the sight of the junk didn't excite me as it used to. It was the work that mattered now.

I decided to go into the house and get acquainted with the birds. I had never been inside before. Feathers and dust burst into the air when I poked my head through the door. The squawking was deafening. I covered my ears and entered. There were cages everywhere — some with several birds, some with just one or two. It wasn't hard to spot the

Kaiser. He was a large, brightly coloured parrot. He followed me with his eyes and stared so intensely I found it unnerving.

I picked up the instructions Ziegfried left and sat down and read them through. Then I went around and gave every bird fresh water and seed. Some received vitamins and fruit. The Kaiser received the most. When he saw me approach with pieces of fruit he rolled his head around in circles and suddenly looked very friendly. But I was careful to keep my fingers away. Ziegfried said he had collected the birds simply by rescuing them from people throwing out old cages. I couldn't imagine it.

Back in the shed I picked up the sander just as the alarm light started blinking. This alerted us when someone drove up to the gate. I put the sander down and went out. A man in a truck looked surprised to see me. I tried my hardest to look disinterested in whatever he had in the back of his truck, which turned out to be old lawn mowers and buckets of bolts. I took a quick peek at the bolts, which I knew Ziegfried would be interested in, and tried to sound bored.

"We can't use any of this."

"Nothing? Where's the other fellah — the big guy."

"He's not here. I could give you fifteen dollars for the metal but . . . we really don't need any of that stuff."

I turned to go. I had seen Ziegfried use this tactic.

"Fifteen bucks? I was hoping to get a little more than that."

"Sorry. We've got more lawn mowers than we can shake a stick at and more bolts than we can count."

I started to go again.

"All right, all right. I've come all this way, I might as well get rid of it."

I opened the gate. He drove in and emptied his truck. I paid him from a wallet Ziegfried left, then went back to the shed. I put on a face-protector and got busy with the tedious work of sanding. An hour later the light started blinking again. I pulled off the mask, shook the dust from my clothes and went to the gate. There I found Mr. Boyd, one of my teachers. In his summer clothes, Mr. Boyd didn't look much like a teacher. He didn't act like one either.

"Is Ziegfried here?"

"Nope."

"You in charge?"

"Yup."

"Okay. We'll, I'm looking for a bathtub — one of those old-fashioned ones. Have you got any of those?"

I squinted up at the sky and pretended I was thinking hard.

"Maybe."

"What do you mean, 'maybe?' Either you've got one or you haven't."

"I think we might have one but they're expensive."

"Okay. But you *do* have one?"

"I might be able to find one."

In truth, we had more than a dozen and Ziegfried would be glad to get rid of them.

Then Boyd let his guard down.

"The thing is: we're renovating the house and the wife has always wanted one of those old tubs and if I come home without one I might as well sleep in the barn."

I grinned. I felt like giving him one for free, but my loyalty to Ziegfried was rock solid.

"It'll cost you fifty dollars. I should be charging sixty but seeing as you're my teacher and all . . ."

"Fifty bucks!"

"It's better than sixty."

"Yah, I guess so. Okay, then. Let me see it first."

"I'll see if I can find it for you. Just wait here."

I slowly sauntered away until I was around the corner of the house. Then I took off as fast as I could and grabbed a trolley and rushed to a back corner where the bathtubs were. The tubs were heavy and I struggled to get one onto the cart and push it across the yard. I paused to catch my breath before coming around the corner of the house.

"You're lucky. We just happened to have one left. And it's a white one. I think I'm supposed to charge seventy-five for this."

"You said *fifty*!"

He took fifty dollars out of his wallet.

I sighed and took the money as if I were doing him a big favour. Then we loaded the tub onto his truck.

"Well, this ought to make her happy."

"I'm glad you won't have to sleep in the barn."

"Me too."

After he left, I grinned all the way back to the shed. I didn't know why Ziegfried hated buying and selling so much. It was fun.

Chapter Five

After a week, Ziegfried came striding into the yard with a big smile, two heavy suitcases and a huge backpack. I could tell the suitcases were heavy the way he held them low to the ground. Ziegfried was probably the strongest man for a thousand miles.

"Alfred! You won't believe it!"

"Is your mother okay?"

"Okay? She'll live to be a hundred and fifty. Hah! Do you know what happened?"

"What?"

"Well, she had written to me in her old scribbled hand-

writing and said she was 'leaving soon' and 'hoped I'd make it to the funeral.' Of course I thought she was talking about herself. But she wasn't. An old great aunt of mine died. My mother was just 'leaving soon' to go to her funeral. Here I go all the way to Germany to see my dying mother, who greets me at the door but has forgotten she even wrote to me by then, and takes one look at me and says: 'What are *you* doing here?'

"Well, I laughed and cried and laughed and cried, and then had a great old time visiting all my relatives. To top it off, the old aunt left me a pile of money. And do you know what, Al? I went to a second-hand marine shop over there and guess what I found?"

"What?"

He opened the suitcases. Wrapped in oiled paper were glass discs, metal plates, gauges, screens, valves, hoses, knobs and wire.

"Nothing . . . but a periscope and sonar."

My mouth dropped.

"A periscope?"

"Well, it *will* be once we construct it. But these are the important pieces."

"Wow. That's lucky."

"It's really lucky. We'd never find this stuff around here. And so, Al, how did you make out here? I see you've still got all your fingers."

I smiled.

"The birds are okay. I sold two bathtubs, a screen door,

a winch, five toilets, a bunch of wire and . . . the old Ford station wagon."

"The old Ford wagon? You sold it?"

"I hope that was okay."

"What did you sell it for?"

"Three hundred and fifty."

"Three hundred and fifty! You got three hundred and fifty for the old Ford wagon? Oh, Al, that's wonderful! And you sold two bathtubs?"

"Yup."

"What were the total sales for the week?"

"Seven hundred and twenty-eight dollars and seventy-five cents."

"Al, that's amazing! I can't believe it. That's absolutely wonderful. Did you buy anything?"

"Some lawn mowers and bolts . . . and a fridge and stove. Altogether I spent forty-five dollars."

"You sold seven hundred and twenty-eight bucks and only spent forty-five?"

"Yup."

"Al, you're a genius."

"I was lucky, I guess."

"Oh no. There's no luck about it. You're a born salesman that's what it is. Seven hundred and twenty-eight bucks . . . in one week. Well, that's something."

By late summer the wood interior was finished. We donned overalls and ventilator masks and painted five coats of

waterproofing varnish into the wood. This gave the interior a golden shine. It was beautiful. There were still many open spaces for the installation of equipment but the interior already looked more or less what it would look like when it was done.

Next, we worked on laying the electrical, gas, air and hydraulic pipes and fittings. This was all wizardry to me. I assisted Ziegfried with a silent awe. Only rarely would he disappear into the house to consult a manual on a specific problem. Otherwise, it looked as if he constructed submarines for a living.

But he insisted upon my understanding how everything worked, and . . . how to fix anything when it broke down. Everything breaks down *sometime*, he said. For every system — both in diagram and actual construction — I learned every step between the switch and the function. Thus, for instance, the engine switch sat on the panel board, which was in the main compartment, right in front of where the stationary bicycle would stand. First, there was the switch itself, which I learned to build from scratch. Then, there were the wires, which ran through waterproofed pipes to the engine itself, stored in its own soundproofed, waterproofed compartment in the stern. Ziegfried went over every detail again and again until I had a crystal-clear picture of the whole system in my mind, and learned how to diagnose a problem by the sound of the engine running. And so it was with all the other systems.

The propulsion of the sub was created by three systems,

either singly or in combination. I could drive the sub simply by running the engine — but only on the surface. The engine required a constant flow of air, which simply wasn't available once the sub dived. Running the engine was the fastest but noisiest way. Completely submerged, the sub could travel by battery alone, which was much quieter, once it had stored enough power by running the engine for awhile; or, I could simply ride the bike. By bicycle gears alone the sub would move about as fast as someone paddling a canoe. At that rate, Ziegfried said, allowing for currents and such, I could cross the Atlantic in about three months. By engine alone I could do it in about two weeks.

But I could run all three systems at once. That is, I could drive the sub by engine power, which stored power in the batteries, and, I could pedal, which would also add juice to the batteries. When fully charged, the batteries might propel the sub for about ten hours or so, depending upon the speed. But this was slower than engine power, and the batteries had to run other functions inside the sub as well.

For fuel, Ziegfried installed two permanent tanks and a small, portable auxiliary tank, which I could carry out of the sub and fill by hand. Altogether, he estimated the sub could travel about three thousand miles before needing to be refuelled. Of course I could lengthen that distance immeasurably by pedalling.

In the evenings, after a full day's work, I went to Deep Cove and practised diving. I could reach fifty feet now fairly com-

fortably and my lung capacity had improved a lot. The trick was slowing everything down. This was a state of mind more than anything else. I would breathe deeply and focus on slowing my heartbeat. Then, instead of hurrying down, I would simply sink past the markers as if I had all the time in the world. I could hold my breath a full minute and a half — three times as long as when I first started. Rarely did my ears bother me anymore. Ziegfried said I was growing webbed feet.

At fifty feet, on a clear day, I could see the schooner below. She lay on her side like a ghost. Just fifty feet more and I would be able to touch her and maybe find something interesting to bring back.

And then one evening I got a terrible fright. It was my last dive for the day. I had reached the fifty-foot marker and paused for a second to stare at the schooner. Suddenly, there was a shadow above me. I looked up. On the surface I saw a shark.

My heart pounded in my chest. I knew there were sharks occasionally caught in fishermen's nets but it wasn't often — we were so far north. I watched the shark glide back and forth as if it were looking for something. My lungs insisted I rise. So, I started to move. I came up as slowly and controlled as possible, trying not to make any sudden movements that might attract the shark's attention. But it never seemed interested in me. It bumped against the wire once and I felt it as if a cow had bumped against a fence. I was surprised at its strength.

When I reached the surface I slowly climbed onto the raft. It was only when I was out of the water that I saw the shark's fin cutting through the water about thirty feet away, and I felt a shiver run through my spine. It came close once more and then disappeared.

Ziegfried couldn't believe it.

"You're braver than anyone I know, Al. You're not afraid to go back?"

"Not really."

Having shared the water with a shark once made me more confident to do it again.

"Well, we can take comfort in the fact that there has never been a shark attack in these waters, or at least not a reported one. People *have* been lost at sea. I suppose no one knows what happened to them. I take my hat off to you, Al. You've got the courage of an explorer, that's for sure."

I appreciated Ziegfried's support. It was a different story at home. My grandfather had noticed I was growing stronger and more confident — changes he didn't expect me to make until I was out on the fishing boat. He had no idea how hard I was already working.

"I'd take you out now," he said, "except that it's a tradition in our family to come out when you're fourteen. I'm afraid you'll just have to wait one more year, Alfred."

All I could think was how the submarine had be ready by the end of the school year — when I turned fourteen. I was already scouting for places in the woods to set up a tent if I had to.

"Once you come out on the boat, you'll forget about everything else. It's in your blood."

By "everything else," I knew he meant the submarine. But he was wrong. I lived and breathed for the day I would go to sea — but not as a fisherman — as an explorer.

Chapter Six

Over the fall we installed the batteries, air-compressors, driveshaft, propeller and stationary bike. There were ten industrial-size batteries — each the size of a small suitcase. The propeller had come from a fancy yacht that had been damaged in a storm years before. The air-compressors were installed independently — each operating as a backup to the other in case of failure. Ziegfried was still working out the design for a manual inflation of the ballast tanks. The stationary bike was an adaptation of an old touring bicycle. It had ten gears, an adjustable seat and toe-clips, for greater pedalling efficiency. I found it extremely easy, but Ziegfried

said this would all change when the sub was sitting in water.

Each installation brought the sub nearer to completion, and my hopes rose every time. But Ziegfried kept talking about how much work there was left to do, and I knew he never said things he didn't mean. Without a functioning sonar system the sub was useless in the water. It was like going down the highway with your eyes closed, he said.

"After all, Al, you won't be the *only* sub in the sea."

The periscope also had to be constructed and installed, as did the heating, lighting, communications and safety systems. And then, every system had to be thoroughly tested. Ziegfried put special emphasis on the testing phase.

"But there is one thing we *can't* test, Al."

"What?"

"The sub's buoyancy. Once we slip her into the water she's *done*, except for minor adjustments. If she sinks like a stone she's gone. We'll never get her out of the water again without a proper landing. And that's a lot of work and we'd have to get a permit to build it and things would get mired in bureaucratic red tape. You can be sure they'd send government people down to inspect the sub, and then it would have to pass a thousand tests and I don't think the sub would ever leave the yard."

"Oh."

I hadn't given any thought to the legal side of things.

"I'm not really worried about the sub sinking, Al. Laws of physics dictate she will float. The ballast we've added gives

us more control, so I feel pretty confident about her overall buoyancy. What I wish we could test is her maneuverability — how she sits in the water and how she rides. Will she ride with her nose up, or down? Will she cut through the water smoothly and with little drag, or will she create waves that slow you down? Will she rock side to side like a bouncing clown and make you seasick before you even leave the harbour? These are things we cannot know until she's in the water."

I continued to dive all through September and October. Diving every day kept my body adjusted to the changing ocean temperature. I felt cold, but it didn't bother me as it used to. I didn't see any more sharks either, but always kept an eye out for them. By mid-October, I was down to sixty feet. On my last dive of the season — Halloween day — I touched the sixty-five-foot marker before surfacing. I was under the water for a minute and forty-five seconds. Ziegfried was deeply impressed.

"That's a heck of a lot of weight sitting on top of you, Al. What does it feel like?"

For once, I felt like *I* was the expert and Ziegfried the novice.

"I don't know. It just feels like something squeezing your whole body together. It's very tight, especially on your chest."

"Well, it compresses your lungs, you know."

"You get used to it."

"And a minute and forty-five seconds without breathing. I can't imagine it. Nerves of steel, Al. Nerves of steel."

I grinned.

In the fall and winter I could only come to the yard after school and on weekends. It was hard to sit through the long days at school. I tried to do my homework while I was there, so I wouldn't have to do it later. By November I was no longer diving and I could also spend my evenings at the yard. My grandfather and grandmother didn't see much of me — only at breakfast and before bed.

"I was the same at his age," said my grandfather. "Never mind. Let him enjoy his freedom; he'll be busy soon enough."

Yes, I said to myself, but not in the way you think. I tried to explain my passion for exploring to my grandfather, but my words fell on deaf ears.

"When you are a child," he said, "it is okay to think like a child. But when you are a man you must think like a man."

I dropped my head. I didn't want to let my grandfather down, but I would die if I had to accept a life on the fishing boats.

"It's a tough situation, Al," said Ziegfried. "It is important to respect our elders, that's for sure. On the other hand, a man has got to do what he has got to do. In the end, it's *your* life. Your grandfather has had his life. Now it's your turn.

But I feel for you, Al. It's not an easy thing to turn your back on your elders."

"I already decided a long time ago. I just wish he would accept it."

"Hmmm. Have you ever actually *told* your grandfather you are decidedly *not* going to be a fisherman?"

"Not exactly."

"Maybe you should."

"I know what he would say."

"You never know for sure. He might surprise you."

I went home and lay awake thinking about it. In the morning I greeted my grandfather, "Grandpa. I have made a firm decision not to become a fisherman."

My grandfather looked out the window.

"Could be a squall this evening," he said.

"I'm sorry, but I'm *not* going to be a fisherman," I repeated.

My grandfather picked up his lunch and rain gear.

"Well, I'm off to the wharf."

I turned and looked at my grandmother. Awkwardly, she caught my eye.

"Don't be late for school," she said suddenly.

I sighed deeply.

"Well," said Ziegfried later, "you tried, Al. You were honest."

"It was like talking to a brick wall."

"When people build up expectations over a long time it

can be pretty hard to lose them. How would you feel if we had to scrap the submarine?"

"Terrible! I would feel absolutely terrible!"

"Me too, Al. But you see what I mean."

"Yes, I see what you mean. But I still think it's not right for my grandfather to decide my life for me."

"Well, with that, Al, I agree. I only hope your grandfather comes to see it that way before it's too late."

We hooked up the periscope in the winter and had fun raising it above the plastic shed and looking out to sea. We took turns spotting ships and fishing boats and even the occasional seal. We also installed the sonar system but couldn't test it until the sub was in the water. Not a day went by that I didn't wonder when that would be, but I never mentioned it. Ziegfried was as anxious as I was; there was no need to share my impatience.

In the winter I trained on the stationary bike. Ziegfried attached weight to the propeller shaft to simulate the drag of water. I got lots of exercise. Ziegfried tried the bike too, but after fifteen minutes he was praising the virtues of engines again. I laughed.

Every dry-dock test we *could* do we *did* do, such as running the engine and charging the batteries, then running the propeller on battery power alone. We also tested the bicycle's capacity for juicing up the batteries, which wasn't exactly thrilling. We discovered it took roughly ten hours of

pedalling to charge the batteries enough to run the sub for one hour. That didn't seem like a fair trade to me, but Ziegfried pointed out that I would be propelling the sub *and* juicing the batteries at the same time, so it was not as bad as it seemed.

In the winter we completed the electrical, heating and lighting systems and tested them. We hooked up a short-wave radio for contact between the sub and junkyard, although I would have to be on the surface to send or receive signals. We sent away for books on navigation, ship-to-ship communication and ocean currents, and we studied and discussed them. I had to learn Morse code and how to read flags. I had no idea I would have to study so much, but Ziegfried said you can't go to sea if you can't communicate in the language of mariners. As with everything else, there was more preparation required, more factors to consider, and more work to do than I ever dreamed. It always seemed endless to me and I feared that the sub, and I, would never leave shore.

But it was not so.

Chapter Seven

By April, the ice was gone and I was down at Deep Cove, sticking my toes in the water, trying to hurry along the warming process. Work on the sub was at a difficult stage for me — the stage of ironing out the kinks. Everything had the appearance of being more or less finished, but this was precisely when Ziegfried was the fussiest, and he meticulously went over the order and functioning of every single item in the sub — with a patience I found painful to observe. There was little for me to do besides study the mariner manuals. If Ziegfried tested a system, and it worked, why would he have to test it again, and again and again? But he was insatiable in his need to test the equipment. I had long

ago learned to bite my tongue, but I couldn't do anything about the painful expression on my face. After all, it was less than two months to the end of school, my fourteenth birthday . . . and my grandfather's expectation of my appearance on his boat. Ziegfried knew all of this, but made it clear the sub would never leave the yard until he was confident everything was in proper working order.

"Do you know why most of the early subs failed?" he said, as he watched the gauges in the air-compressors rise during a test and I sat behind him and fidgeted nervously with my hands.

"Lack of testing?"

He shook his head.

"Leaky valves. The builders just didn't know enough about water pressure. They constructed valves that couldn't take the wear and tear of the sea. Many sailors lost their lives because of a space between fittings no thicker than a quarter. I've read all about it. There's no room for error, Al. As they say at the American submarine academy, the sea doesn't care if you are sincere."

I knew he was always right about these things; it was just so difficult when the deadline was so close.

On the 1st of May, Ziegfried gave me an early birthday present. I came into the yard after school and saw a box with ribbons resting on the stationary bike.

"What's that?"

"A present."

"For who?"

"For you."

"But it's not my birthday."

"It will be. Anyway, you need it now. Go ahead. Open it."

I tore off the ribbon and opened it up. Inside was a black spongy suit; feet, gloves and headpiece fell out.

"What's this?"

"A wetsuit."

My eyes opened wide.

"A wetsuit! Wow! Hey! I could go diving right now. I won't get too cold. Wow! Thank you. I don't know what to say."

"Don't say anything. Go down to the water and try it out. Take the belt that's hanging on the chair. Without that you won't sink. That suit is pure buoyancy."

"I will. Thank you so much. It is the nicest present I ever received."

"Don't mention it."

I took the suit and belt and hurried down to Deep Cove. It took nearly half an hour to get into the suit the first time. Then I couldn't hear anything but my own breathing. It was so stiff I felt like a space man walking across the beach. I stepped out over the stones and let the icy water soak into the suit. At first it was very cold, but warmed up quickly with my body's heat. As the suit absorbed water it lost its stiffness and I could move freely about. With a grin I started to swim towards the drop-off.

The water was about ten feet deep. I was so enjoying the wetsuit that I never bothered to look ahead, and nearly

swam straight into something big and black. I lifted my head just three feet away and got the biggest scare of my life. For once, I really panicked. I spun around and raced back to shore as fast as I could. I reached the shallows and ran up the beach, not the least bit careful where my feet landed. I turned around and stared at the water. Nothing had followed me. Then, ever so slightly, I saw a swelling just beneath the surface. It wasn't moving, but the waves cresting over it revealed a large mass. I climbed the bluff to take a better look.

Something was in the water but it was not moving by itself. Likely, it was dead. By its size it looked like a whale. Whales had washed up in other places. This must have been what it was.

What a fright it had given me. How disappointing to have panicked. That didn't seem like the thing an explorer would do. I was so proud that Ziegfried thought I was brave. Here now, I had run out of the ocean like a chicken. I wanted to redeem myself, but, in truth, I was afraid to go back in the water.

I've got to do this, I thought. What explorer is afraid of a dead whale?

For fifteen minutes I just stared, hoping the whale would wash up by itself. But it didn't. Okay, I thought. I can do this. I am going to swim out there and look at that whale and do my diving just as I planned.

I immersed again and started to swim slowly towards the whale. My heart beat loudly at all kinds of unhappy possi-

bilities. Perhaps the whale was not dead, just sleeping. Perhaps it would grab me and carry me out to sea. I knew that wasn't very realistic; whales were gentle creatures. At least that's what you always heard.

Fifty feet away it looked enormous. My heart beat so loudly I had to stop. Suddenly the thought of riding around in a tiny submarine through the vast, dark ocean seemed a lot more dangerous. But a huge sense of disappointment came over me when I thought that, so I swam a little closer, then stopped and listened to my heart pounding. I swam a few feet closer, then stopped. A few feet more and stopped again. Now I could see the whole whale clearly. Probably it was dead, but what if it were just sleeping and I startled it awake and it accidentally crushed me against the rocks trying to escape the shallow water? I decided to swim around it. But which end, the head or tail? I chose the tail.

As I went around the whale I was suddenly filled with sadness. It was almost as if I were staring at a dead person. On the other side, I stopped and stared for about five minutes. I was happy for having conquered my fear, but felt terribly sorry for the whale.

At the drop-off, the wire was still attached to the buoy. I breathed deeply and dove to fifty feet without any trouble. But the wetsuit was tricky: one minute you were warm enough; the next, an icy shiver rushed through your body. After two more dives I decided it was enough excitement for one day.

On the way back in, I swam right up to the whale and touched it. Its skin was hard, not soft and rubbery at all, but hard, like wood, and scaly, with barnacles. I swam around the head but got a fright at one of its eyes. It was dead, surely, but something about its eye spooked me — its wildness maybe, or perhaps because it came from the depths of another world. I felt deeply sorry for it, and told it so, then swam back to shore.

I went back to see Ziegfried before going home. He felt sad for the whale, too, he said, but was more surprised I had gone back out.

"All by yourself? You went back out all by yourself and touched the whale and everything?"

He shook his head back and forth.

"You're as bold as a man could be, Al. It's no wonder your soul rebels at the idea of working on a fishing boat — you've got greater things in you, much greater things."

I smiled.

"The wetsuit is really nice."

"I'm glad. I give you a wetsuit and you go out and find a whale. Hah!"

"But I'm worried that people will see the whale on the beach," I said, "and take an interest in Deep Cove — just at the time we might be wanting to launch the sub."

I studied his face for any reaction to the suggestion the sub might be ready that soon.

"Well, yes, you're right. They will certainly see the whale.

And yes, it could become a problem for us if people start hanging around the cove. There are other places to launch the sub, I suppose, but none so close. But let's not worry too much about what *might* happen. Let's deal with what happens when it does."

I agreed. At least he was concerned about the launching.

Chapter Eight

The whale washed up on the beach and drew lots of attention. Crews came from TV stations and interviewed local fishermen and filmed everything. I watched the filming on the beach, then saw it on the news, where, to my surprise, everything was changed. In the first place, Deep Cove was an isolated, rocky cove where no one ever went, except me. On TV they made it look like a favourite beach. They suggested the fishermen spent weekends there with their families. I had to laugh; none of the fishermen could even swim.

Then, just as I feared, people talked about the schooner

and made it sound like more than it was. She went down in a terrible storm hundreds of years ago, they said. Many people lost their lives. I knew that no one had died. Worst of all: they said the schooner was carrying a secret cargo but was sunken so deep and was surrounded by such a terrible undertow it was impossible to reach her. One fisherman said that nobody knew how deep the ocean was at Deep Cove but it was probably unfathomable. Another hinted that maybe the Loch Ness monster was down there. I burst out laughing when I heard that. But what really surprised me was how the TV gave as much attention to the deep and mysterious cove and its sunken ship — which was mostly untrue — as it did to the dead whale on the beach, which *was* true.

For a few weeks there were people hanging around the cove, which was frustrating. I had to dive early in the mornings, before school. For a few days I couldn't dive at all, because the fishermen had to cut up the whale. Otherwise, it would rot and the cove would stink terribly all summer. So I waited until the whale was butchered and the tide washed the beach clean.

May passed so slowly it was painful. Then, in the first week of June, my grandfather gave me an early birthday present and told me to open it right away so I could get used to it — a pair of boots for the fishing boat. I said thank you quietly and put the boots in my room.

"You'd better wear those boots around for a week or two," he said, "so that you're good and used to them."

I just dropped my head. In the second week of June I carried my tent out to the woods and cleared a space for fires. I didn't tell anyone, not even Ziegfried. Every day I dropped off a few cans of food and spare clothes and my sleeping bag. I took a large waterproof tarp from the junkyard and hung it above the tent to ensure complete dryness. Lastly, I brought out a radio and my mariner manuals.

In the third week of June, school ended and I turned fourteen. On Sunday, my grandfather told me to get to bed early because we would go fishing first thing in the morning. I felt stomach-sick all day. In the evening I returned to the house, wrote my grandparents a long letter in which I thanked them for all the love and care they had given me all those years. I apologized for leaving and hoped they would forgive me for following a life of my own choosing. I concluded by promising to write letters regularly and to come back and visit before long. I left the letter on my bed and went out to the woods.

During the first night I could hardly sleep. I made a fire and a pot of tea and sat and poked the coals with a stick. I thought of all the adventures lying ahead of me. I wanted to sail every ocean and explore every island and continent. It would be dangerous sometimes, I knew. I might even die young through some unforeseen accident, or at the hands of modern-day pirates, but as I stared into the dancing

flames I felt a wonderful certainty for the direction I had chosen for my life.

In the morning I went to the junkyard as usual. Ziegfried was installing a tiny electric motor to retract a floatable cable that would serve as a radio antenna when the sub was submerged. He knew it was the day I was expected on the fishing boat and he eyed me closely, but didn't say anything. Neither did I. I knew it was important to show that my actions were my own.

On the second day it was different. I had taken a long time to get to sleep, then slept in. So it was much later than usual when I showed up at the yard. Ziegfried was fashioning a small anchor for the sub. When he saw me he breathed a sigh of relief.

"Sleep in, Al?"

I yawned and stretched.

"Yup. But I had the best sleep of my life last night."

"Did you now? How's that?"

"I set up my tent in the woods. It's really cozy. You wouldn't believe how many shooting stars there are in one night."

"Your grandfather came around earlier."

"He did?"

"Yup. Said he figured you were staying here."

"What did you say?"

"I said I thought you were camping out in the woods. I guess I was right."

I stared at the ground. I didn't know what to say.

"I told him I'd keep an eye on you."

"You did? Thank you."

"You're welcome. I was thinking, Al."

"Yes?"

He looked stern.

"I was thinking . . . we could launch in August. What do you think?"

Excitement raced through me like a lightning bolt.

"I think that sounds pretty good."

"Well, there are a million things to do, of course. The truth is, many of the systems need to be tested in the water. Only then will we know for sure if she's seaworthy."

I nodded. "The water's nice and warm in August. We can spend lots of time in and out of the sub while we're testing her."

"That we will, Al."

By July, I was diving in the afternoons again. There were no traces of the whale, or tourists, except for a little garbage on the beach. I had gotten used to the wetsuit but didn't need it anymore, or the raft. Now I could swim out to the buoy, breathe deeply and dive to seventy-five feet — without stones. I descended at a calm, steady rate and could stay under water for two full minutes. This would have seemed impossible a couple of years before.

At seventy-five feet the schooner was so close. The un-

opened boxes on its deck lay waiting for me to grab, but I could dive no deeper. Any more and it felt like my chest would cave in. But it was exciting to look up and see the surface so far away. And two minutes underwater made me feel like a merman. It also gave me a significant advantage in dealing with dangerous situations.

In July, Ziegfried was working feverishly hard on back-up systems to back-up systems. It was hard not to think he was overdoing it. His latest idea was an automatic inflation of the ballast tanks if the sub should suddenly plunge below 225 feet. A pressure gauge fitted to the outside of the sub would trigger a switch inside, the tanks would automatically fill and the sub would rise. But he couldn't test it.

"I'm not sure, Al. Maybe we should set the depth at 250. I think the sub will take it, what do you think?"

"Twenty-five feet is not a big difference."

In truth, I didn't know what to say. He always seemed to judge on the side of being too cautious. There were so *many* safety features, and I understood how they all worked and could fix them mostly, if necessary. All that remained was to get the sub into the water and try everything out.

"Maybe we'll split the difference," he said, "and set the gauge at 237.5 feet."

"That's a good idea. Then we can test it."

"Oh, you bet we will test it."

Also in July, we built a trailer for transporting the sub. It had fourteen wheels and was cumbersome and unsightly and existed for one function only: to get the sub into the

water. After that, it would be dismantled. The sub was either a success or a failure. Either way it would stay in the ocean. We made no preparations for bringing it back to the yard.

A whole month had passed since I left my grandparents. I half expected to see my grandfather at the junkyard again but he never came. After two weeks I sent them a letter telling them I was fine, doing well, and still around.

The tent had become my home and I was quite comfortable there. I lived on peanut-butter sandwiches, oranges and canned soup — the kind of diet I was planning to eat in the sub. My laundry was a different story. I was used to finding clean clothes on my bed every other day. Now I was starting to realize that if I didn't wash my clothes, nobody else would. I tried to ignore the issue but after a few weeks Ziegfried started bringing it up. I felt a little insulted when he said I smelled like the inside of an old can of paint.

"How do you keep *your* clothes clean?" I asked.

"It may come as a surprise to you, Al, but I wash them all by myself."

So, I borrowed some soap from him and washed my clothes in the stream next to my tent. At first it seemed a terrible waste of time, but once the clothes were dry and I put them on clean, I felt a small, pleasurable sense of satisfaction.

"Well, now there's something," Ziegfried said the next day. "Every sailor washes his own clothes. Good morning, sailor."

"Good morning yourself."

Chapter Nine

The launch took place at Deep Cove in the middle of the night beneath an overcast sky and crescent moon. We wrapped the sub in brown canvas tarps, raised it one end at a time and slid the trailer beneath it. We worked quickly — it was dark at ten o'clock and light again by five. The fishermen would be going to the wharf by four and would see us once they were on the water and the sun came up. We had to drive at a snail's pace over the potholes in the road. Anyone on the road in the middle of night would certainly have seen us, and tongues would wag.

"Murphy's Law, Al: if anything can go wrong, it will."

But other than one flat tire, which didn't stop us, everything went rather well. We reached the cove by two o'clock. Going down the hill was the hardest part. Ziegfried drove his old four-wheel-drive, which had no trouble pulling the trailer on the flat road but struggled backing down the hill. The trailer dragged the truck down whether it wanted to go or not. The trailer tires were only half filled with air so they would absorb many of the bumps without disturbing the balance and help keep us from sinking in the sand. We were afraid more than once that the sub would get stranded on the beach and the fishermen would spy it from their boats.

"We should have borrowed a tractor," Ziegfried said.

It took half an hour to cross the beach where the sand slanted downwards and we could ease into the water. Ziegfried backed up until the trailer was completely submerged. I pulled the tarps off and secured a rope from the sub to the truck. Together, we entered the water, climbed on top of the sub and unlashed it from the trailer. Gently, like a tamed whale, the sub floated free of the trailer. We yelled with excitement.

"Woo . . . Hooooo! Woo . . . Hooooo!"

The sub rocked slightly from side to side but did not drop its bow or stern, and did not sink.

"She sits well in the water, Al. She sits very well indeed."

I was too excited to speak. I just wanted to jump inside and start the engine and race out to sea. But that would have to wait.

"Okay, Al. I'll take the truck up the hill and hide the trailer. Why don't you climb inside and throw a few switches?"

He slipped off the sub and clambered up the beach to the truck. I opened the hatch of the portal and climbed inside. Everything was familiar, yet different. The sub seemed tiny compared to its size in the yard. And whereas before it sat perfectly still, now it rocked gently in the waves. This gave it a whole new feeling.

I took my seat in front of the control panel and flipped the switches to activate the electrical system. The sub filled with light — soft, white, over-head lights, and blue, green, orange lights on the sonar, radar and pressure systems. I wanted to wait until Ziegfried came back before starting the engine; it was such a special moment.

I didn't have to wait long. There was a slight tilt to one side as he climbed the side of the sub. Next, water spilled inside from his clothes. I watched the water run into the drain. One peek at the panel board told me the flush tank was registering a marginal amount of water.

Ziegfried came down the ladder, and, with a beaming face took a seat on the floor. He was too tall to stand in the sub.

"Well, Captain?"

It came as a surprise to me. But it was true; *I* was the captain of the sub. I was the one who would sail it. By the law of the sea, this made me the captain.

"I think we should start the engine."

Ziegfried nodded respectfully as I reached over and flipped the engine switch. We heard it ignite in the stern and felt a soft purring vibration come up through the floor. We grinned at each other with satisfaction.

"I see there is water in the flush tank, Captain. Do you think we ought to flush it?"

"Yes, I think so."

I flipped another switch. A small hissing sound was heard as pressurized air was blown into the tank. The panel board read that the tank was now empty. Everything was working like a dream.

"And now?" said Ziegfried.

He looked at his watch. I glanced at the clock on the control panel. It was three thirty. The fishermen would be on the wharf in half an hour and out in their boats not long after that.

"We need to tie up out of sight," I said.

"What do you suggest?"

To the right was a smaller cove where the sub could blend in with jutting rocks.

"Let's go around the corner and keep an eye on the sonar to make sure we don't hit anything."

"Aye, aye, Captain."

I laughed. Ziegfried made an unlikely first mate.

The sonar revealed a flat bottom with a series of rising columns to the right. Some of these broke through the sur-

face. Underwater they spread out onto the ocean floor. I put the sub in first gear and took hold of the throttle. As I raised the throttle the engine purred more loudly and the sub began to move forward. Watching the sonar, I carefully steered between the rocks. After cutting the engine, we drifted slowly.

"If you reverse the engine a tiny bit when you want to stop," said Ziegfried, "you should be able to cause the sub to sit still. This is what the fishermen do."

I put the engine in reverse and raised the throttle. The reversing of the propeller caused water turbulence and the sub rocked gently from side to side, but stopped moving forward. I shut the engine off.

"She's very responsive, Captain. Excellent."

We climbed out of the hatch and looked around. The sub was neatly placed between three jutting rocks.

"It's a good place," said Ziegfried. "They won't see her from out there. Now if we tie her up she won't bang against the rocks."

So we moored the sub and dropped our small anchor overboard and watched a thin line of blue appear on the horizon.

"Okay, Al. We should get some sleep. Are you going to stay in the sub?"

"You bet."

"Okay. I'll be back in the afternoon. It's been quite a night."

We shook hands. Then Ziegfried slipped into the water and climbed up on a rock.

"Maybe we should take a peek at that schooner tomorrow," he said as he disappeared out of sight.

My bed was a hanging cot — a narrow metal basket with a foam mattress, suspended in the air by bungee cords. The cords permitted the cot to swing level when the sub was tossing and turning — a preventative against seasickness. I poked around for awhile, peered out the periscope, then climbed into bed and curled up in the blankets. The wall floated gently up and down with the waves as I fell asleep. I slept long and peacefully and didn't wake until Ziegfried's booming voice came through the portal.

"Ahoy! Captain! Permission to come aboard?"

I swung out of bed and climbed the portal. Ziegfried was stretched between a rock and the sub, holding a bag above his head with one hand.

"I brought pizza and root-beer. A celebration."

I wiped the sleep from my eyes.

"Good morning."

"Good afternoon."

"Good afternoon. You brought pizza?"

"Yup."

He handed the bag over and climbed up the sub.

"Thanks. I guess I slept a long time."

"You know what, Al? We should bring a small rubber

dinghy down here and hide it somewhere. Then we won't have to get soaked every time we come to the sub."

"Good idea. Thanks for the pizza. I'm really hungry."

"Well, I thought you might be. Let's eat. We have a lot to test today."

After a celebratory lunch we untied the sub and started it up and took it over to the drop-off. I watched the sonar while Ziegfried scrunched up in the observation window.

"I see the wire! And I think maybe I see the schooner. Wow, Al, that's a long way down. I can't believe you dove most of the way down there."

"It's not so hard, once you get used to it."

"If you're a fish. Okay, if we secure the hatch we can make our first test dive. What do you think, Captain?"

I grinned.

"You bet!"

"You should do it all by yourself, Al. Just pretend I'm not here."

"Okay."

I climbed the portal and sealed the hatch, then returned to my seat and examined the control panel. Flipping four switches let water into four ballast compartments at the same time. The depth gauge told us the sub was sinking.

"We're going down, Al. Can you feel it?"

"Yes."

"I can see the schooner more clearly. Be careful we don't hit bottom."

At seventy-five feet I pumped a little air into the ballast tanks. The sub slowed but didn't stop.

"More air, Al! We're still falling! More air!"

I added more air. The sub slowed again but the depth gauge read ninety-five feet.

"We're right beside the schooner, Al! We're going to hit!"

There was gentle but loud bump as the sub touched the ocean floor.

"Ooops!" I said.

"Yikes! Well, it wasn't too bad. I don't think we did any damage. But that shows how tricky it is to dive."

I looked at the depth gauge.

"We're rising!"

"I know. Now you've got to let more water into the tanks again. But just a little, Al. It'll take awhile to get the hang of it. That's why we're testing."

"At least we know everything works."

"That's right. More importantly . . . no leaks!"

I smiled. I knew there wouldn't be any leaks.

All afternoon we practised diving and surfacing. I began to get a feeling for how much air was needed, and, when to let it in or out. Timing was everything. Learning to control the sub, Ziegfried said, was like trying to teach an elephant tricks in the circus. A lot of patience was required to learn the smallest skill.

On one of our dives we sat right above the schooner and stared.

"She's pretty big, Al. I'd say, fifty feet or so."

"What do you think is in those boxes?"

"Who knows? Could be anything: wine, thumbtacks, silverware . . . books."

"Treasure?"

"No, not on the deck. If a ship were carrying treasure it would be hidden somewhere. It's probably something ordinary, and probably ruined by the salt water anyway."

"Do you think we could raise one and have a look?"

"You're the captain. I'm just the technical support. If you say, 'raise those boxes,' then I'll get busy and figure out how to do it."

I laughed.

"I'd *love* to get our hands on one."

"Me too. Well, I have an idea. But I think we'd have to secure the services of a good open-water diver."

"I think I can find one."

The next day we dropped a cable with a hook-basket. When the basket was lowered onto a box, the hooks would grip around the edges and tighten up. Then we could raise it. But I needed to swim close enough to place the basket by hand.

Ziegfried took the sub down to sixty feet. He brought the basket as close to a box as possible. Then, I swam down to seventy-five feet and fiddled with the cable until the basket fell over one of the boxes. It took three dives to get it in place. Looking at Ziegfried from outside the observation

window was the funniest feeling; I could hardly concentrate. But I did hook one box and we pulled it up with the sub.

The box was too heavy to hoist out of the water but we pulled it alongside the sub and tied it up. Then we took the sub close to a rock with a flat edge to use as a landing. With ropes we managed to pull the box onto the rock.

"Whew!" said Ziegfried. "This better be worth it. There better be diamonds inside."

"Or gold."

I fetched a hammer from the sub's toolbox and Ziegfried tore the box open. The two of us stared inside and burst out laughing.

"Sardines!"

The boxes were full of sardines. Our first treasure. We laughed until our stomachs ached.

Chapter Ten

The rest of the summer was spent checking off a list of tests — diving and surfacing tests, engine tests, battery tests, sonar tests, bicycle tests — night and day. We tested how fast the sub could go and how quickly it could stop. We lowered listening sensors into the water from the beach and tested how much noise the sub made on its various maneuvers. We made sighting tests by standing on shore with a pair of binoculars. Ziegfried said the sub looked like a peanut floating on top of a pot of soup. Then, just when I thought maybe he had exhausted his list of tests, he began his *secret* tests.

We were preparing for deeper water. Ziegfried, who had

been fiddling in the stern, sat on the floor and waited for me to start the engine. I flipped the engine switch, but . . . nothing happened. I flipped it again.

"Nothing's happening!"

"Oh?" he said, looking innocent. "I wonder what's wrong."

I stared at him and suddenly realized what was going on. He had intentionally sabotaged the sub. It was up to me to find the problem and fix it. I had to be quick too. What if the engine broke down when pirates were chasing me?

I opened the panel board and checked the engine switch. It seemed okay. I followed the wiring through its water-proof piping to the stern. It was next to impossible to have a break in the wiring within the piping. Likely the problem was in the engine compartment. I checked the wires to the starter — they seemed okay at a glance. I checked the spark plugs and every visible working component. Everything was sparkling clean and in perfect working order. I shook my head and went back to the control panel and flipped the switch again. Nothing.

"What can it be?"

Ziegfried shrugged his shoulders.

"Don't ask me. I'm a thousand miles away."

I went through the sequence again. The switch was fine, the starter was fine, the wires seemed okay, the engine was perfect.

"It doesn't make sense."

I checked the fuel line. It was okay. I came back to the panel board and shook my head.

"We're dead in the water, Al."

"I can't figure it out. Everything is okay."

"Everything *is* okay, or, everything *seems* okay?"

That was a clue. Everything *seemed* okay, but something wasn't. I went through the sequence again, with extra care. I examined the switch for looseness when I flicked it. I went back to the engine and checked the wires leading to the starter. They looked perfect. But this time I ran my finger gently underneath them just to be extra sure. Suddenly, one of the wires revealed it was severed in two. It looked normal enough but had been cut right through. I smiled.

"Find something, Al?"

"Maybe."

I went to the toolbox and grabbed pliers and electrician's tape. I bared the wire, spliced it, taped it, then went back and flipped the switch. The engine roared to life.

"Good job, Al! That took you . . . twelve minutes."

"I should have been faster."

"What did you learn?"

"To be more thorough the first time."

"Absolutely! Leave no wire unchecked. Make your first check as thoroughly as possible. Don't let appearances deceive you."

The lesson was not wasted on me. Neither were the many more secret tests he conducted, such as disconnecting hoses, removing electrical plates, loosening switches and valves . . . even hiding my lunch. By the end of summer my patience had been tested as much as anything else. Every time I

wanted to perform a maneuver in the sub it seemed something was broken down. It was a frustrating but invaluable method of teaching. But the biggest test was yet to come.

It was a dark and misty day. We moored the sub close to a rocky promontory in twenty feet of water, above sand, and shut everything off. Ziegfried tied fishing line to the ballast switches and we climbed out, leaving the hatch wide open. Sitting on the rock, we went over the procedure again and again, and then Ziegfried pulled the line. Water was let into the tanks. It gave me a terrible feeling in my stomach to watch the sub begin to dive and water spill inside. The sub went down like a stone. Various compartments, such as the engine room, were sealed watertight, as they normally would have been. Ziegfried looked at his watch.

"Okay, Al. Are you ready?"

I was already breathing deeply. I nodded.

"You've got two minutes. Go!"

I slipped into the water with practised calm. The calmer I was, the more time I had. I swam the short distance to the sub and went headfirst into the portal. It was upsetting to see everything underwater. Once inside, I sealed the hatch, then had to fight down a feeling of panic at the knowledge I was locked inside a tank full of water, under the ocean. Swimming inside, I reached down to the control panel but found myself disoriented. I was backwards and upside down in front of the panel. Again I had to fight down a panic. I shut my eyes.

"Concentrate! Get a grip!"

I opened my eyes, reached for the ballast switches and pulled them. I heard the movement of pressurized air. The sump pumps had also engaged, as they were designed to do. I felt like crying with happiness, but was far from finished. The pumps could not remove enough water quickly enough to save me from drowning. Swimming back up, I unlocked the hatch, climbed out and sealed it again. I swam to the surface, raised my head and took a deep breath of air. That's when I heard Ziegfried yell, "Yay! Way to go, Alfred! Way to go. Yippee!"

I couldn't help myself: "Yahoo!"

"One minute thirty-seven seconds, Al. And let me tell you, that was the longest minute-and-thirty-seven seconds of my life. I was ready to go in after you, Al. I was ready!"

I swam over to the rock. Ziegfried gave me a hand and pulled me up. Then, without warning, he gave me a big bear hug.

"You make me proud, Al. You make me proud. If ever I had a son I would want him to be just like you."

I felt tears start in my eyes but forced them back. I did not want Ziegfried to see me cry. Inside, I was deeply happy. Ziegfried had become the father I had never had.

The sump pumps did what they were designed to do and removed the water from the sub. The sub then rose back to the surface. We climbed in to survey any damage. All of the watertight compartments were intact. But the flood left salt

stains everywhere and Ziegfried suggested we wipe everything down with fresh water. I had removed my bedding, books, clothing and anything I didn't want to get wet. In a real flooding emergency I would just have to dry those things out. At least now we knew it was possible to survive such an ordeal should it ever happen. But what if the sub sank in deep water? At 237.5 feet the ballast tanks would fill. Would that be sufficient to raise the sub if it were filled with water? No, Ziegfried said, the sump pumps could never keep up with water rushing in through an open portal. The hatch would have to be shut. This led him to consider a system for the automatic sealing of the hatch. I sighed at the thought of any more delays.

"It's too important, Al, It might save your life someday. What if a passing ship swamped the sub while the hatch was open? What if you got caught in a hurricane?"

"I would seal it."

"What if you couldn't? What if you were sleeping? What if you were sick or wounded?"

I shrugged my shoulders. Sometimes it was so difficult to accept Ziegfried's cautious wisdom.

In September I took practice runs in the sub while Ziegfried stayed in the yard and worked on the new hatch system. He installed a small motor charged solely with shutting and sealing the hatch when there was water collecting inside the sub. The system could also be operated from a switch on the panel board. This turned out to be an excellent fea-

ture as it allowed me to shut the hatch and dive without leaving my seat at the controls. Now I could dive almost instantly.

But, like everything else, the system had to be tested. This meant we had to flood the sub again — in deeper water.

We decided to sink the sub at Deep Cove, next to the schooner. We set the automatic ballast inflation depth at sixty-five feet and the automatic hatch sealing at six inches of water. Ziegfried placed sensors above the floor that would detect water once it had risen to six inches. The plan was for me to sink the sub and hold onto the outside of it as it went down. On the way down I could observe if the ballast tanks had engaged and watch the hatch close. At seventy-five feet I would let go and return to the surface and wait for the sub to come back up by itself. This could take a while because the sump pumps had to remove enough water to make the sub buoyant again. It was a critical amount of time in the case of an emergency where I might be in freezing water, waiting for the sub to resurface.

There was less stress involved in this sinking because I was never going to be inside when the sub was going down. I simply opened the tanks enough for a slow dive, then climbed out and sat on top while the sub gently submerged and water rushed inside. Holding onto a handle, I took a few deep breaths just before the sub pulled me under. At the last second I looked to the beach and saw Ziegfried waving. I stuck my hand up in the air as the sub pulled me down.

The hatch closed quickly but a lot more than six inches of water got in before it shut. At fifty feet it was still falling and I was afraid it was going to hit bottom too hard and get damaged. At sixty-five feet I heard pressurized air but the sub was not slowing down yet. At seventy-five feet I let go. As I came up I stared down at the sub. It appeared to be slowing down. When I reached thirty feet I saw a cloud of sand burst from beneath the sub. Well, if it hit bottom at the same speed I was rising that wasn't too bad.

Breaking the surface, I waved to Ziegfried. I saw him check his watch.

"Anything happening?"

"I don't know."

I swam to shore to wait. Sitting on the beach together we stared at the buoy, holding our breath.

"We'll be able to tell how much water got in by the water-marks," Ziegfried said.

"How much do you think got in?"

"I don't know . . . two, maybe three feet. How fast did it fall?"

"Pretty fast."

"Hmmm. Maybe four."

He stared at his watch. We both sighed. Suddenly the portal broke the surface.

"Yay!"

"Seventeen minutes, Al."

I swam out and climbed onto the sub. Opening the hatch,

I looked inside and saw several inches of water still swirling and heard the sump pumps going full blast. I read the watermark on the wall: three and a half feet. If I had been inside I would have survived. It would not be a nice experience to be trapped in a sinking sub that's filling with water, but, provided the automatic hatch and automatic ballast inflation systems were functioning properly, I would survive.

Sticking my head out of the hatch, I yelled, "Three and a half!"

"Yes!" exclaimed Ziegfried, and he did a little dance on the beach.

I laughed. Then took a deep breath and sighed happily. The tests were finally over.

Chapter Eleven

On the First of October, beneath a full moon and broken cloud, I went to sea. The ocean was strangely calm. It was like crossing a lake. But further from land, the swells began to grow. I sailed on top with the hatch open. Since most of the sub rode beneath the surface, it cut through the waves more easily than a fishing boat.

I had packed food for three months and fuel for three thousand miles — depending upon how much pedalling I did. My plan was to sail clockwise around Newfoundland, and work south around the Avalon Peninsula, then follow the ferry over to Nova Scotia. I hoped to sail as far south as

Halifax, and, if time permitted, out to Sable Island. I had daydreams of stepping onto the beach there and taking a peek at the island's famous ponies. I would return before the ice. Ziegfried called it "The Grand Tour of the Maritimes," and asked only that I keep a written log of my adventures that he could read at Christmas time. He gave me another one of his great bear hugs when we said goodbye.

Twenty miles from shore I shut the engine off. A look through the periscope revealed nothing in the dark. Nothing appeared on the radar. Turning on the radio, I found a station that played nice music. Climbing onto the bicycle I began to pedal. My plan was to pedal for two hours, two or three times a day, and work up to a total of ten hours. That would earn one hour of battery power.

After two hours, a peek through the periscope showed the sun coming up. Still nothing showed on the radar. The sonar revealed the ocean floor four hundred feet below. I made a cup of tea and opened a can of peaches for breakfast and was about to climb the portal to watch the sun rise when the radar beeped. Startled, I watched as the screen revealed an object coming in my direction. It was about ten nautical miles away. Taking the binoculars, I climbed the portal and scanned the horizon. There it was — a ship, coming towards me. Likely she was a freighter. Maybe she was coming from Iceland. As I didn't have the engine running and wasn't moving, I didn't know if the ship could detect me or not. Once I started the engine she certainly

would. I thought of calling Ziegfried on the short-wave radio and asking his advice. But he was probably sleeping. Besides, I had to learn to make decisions like that on my own.

The freighter was coming straight on. Maybe she would pass closely. Maybe I should pedal out of the way, or, maybe I should dive and let her pass over me. I went down and took another look at the radar. The ship was eight miles away now. She seemed to be moving pretty fast. I went back up and peered through the binoculars again. Yes, she was a freighter. And she was pretty big. I wondered how deeply I should dive.

Going back inside, I watched the radar indicate the ship was six miles away and closing. It was time to make a decision. Flipping the automatic hatch switch, I waited until it sealed, then let water into the tanks. The sub started to dive. As I went down I watched the ship close in on the sonar. At one hundred feet I stopped and sat still and waited. The ship came directly towards me. I had the eerie feeling she was chasing me.

But she wasn't. She passed right over my head and kept on going. I heard the roar of her engines loud and clear, as if they were in the next room. As soon as she was a mile away I surfaced. I wanted to get a look at her from behind. Breaking the surface, I opened the hatch and looked out. With binoculars I could tell from the stern and flags that she was a Greek-owned vessel sailing from Norway. Likely

she was carrying wood products to St. John's, or Halifax, or the eastern U.S.

I waited until she was ten miles past before starting up the engine. The sun had risen and revealed a sky of broken cloud. I set a course for the northeastern corner of New-foundland — a tiny group of islands known as "Little Fogo Islands." It looked like a quiet spot where I could dive beneath the current and catch some sleep.

By mid-morning I reached them. Sailing in between the islands, I watched the ocean floor rise to seventy-five feet. I climbed out, dropped a line overboard and measured the current. I shut the engine, dove to fifty feet, yawned and stretched. The nice thing about a sub was that you could make it as dark as you liked any time of day. All the same, I left a faint light on and climbed into bed. I also left the radio on, with its floating antenna. It felt nice having the sound of voices. Curling up in my blankets, I listened to the radio and drifted off to sleep.

Waking in the late afternoon, I rose to the surface and opened the hatch. I made a cup of tea and peeled an orange and turned on the short-wave radio. Maybe Ziegfried was trying to reach me. He was.

"Alfred!" came Ziegfried's voice, crackled and broken. "There's . . . storm coming . . . by morning . . . things going? Over."

"I'm in the Little Fogo Islands. Everything's going great! Over."

"... high winds and heavy rain, ... the hatch ... waves ... okay?"

"Okay," I said.

"... listen to the radio."

"I *am* listening to the radio."

I finished breakfast and listened to the weather station. A big storm *was* coming. Recreational boaters were advised to stay off the water. Fishermen too. I was excited. I wanted to witness a storm at sea. If things got too wild on the surface, I could simply go beneath. At a hundred feet you wouldn't even be able to tell there *was* a storm.

I charted a course towards Cape Bonavista, past Deadman's Bay. It could take anywhere from seven to ten hours, depending upon the current, and the storm.

The sky grew progressively darker when I left the shelter of the islands, and the ocean churned itself into massive swells. They washed over all but the very top of the portal. I rode with the hatch open for an hour. I wanted to travel as far as possible before diving. If I had to sail by battery I wouldn't make it to Cape Bonavista the same day. As the waves crested, water began to splash inside and engage the sump pumps. It began to rain. The sub rose and fell like a bucking horse. It was exciting. And then, I got a terrible fright.

I was leaning towards the stern because the back of the sub would rise clear out of the water as the bow went into a trough, and the propeller would spin with a strange whis-

tling sound. I was leaning out of the hatch, straining to see, when a large wave struck and lifted me right out of the portal! I never had a chance. All I could do was grab a handle and hang on as my whole body was thrown against the side. The sub promptly dove beneath the next swell and took me with it.

It happened so fast, I never had a chance to think. I just held on, then reached up with my other hand and pulled myself up. My arm was full of pain. It was at least sprained, if not broken. With considerable difficulty I reached the hatch and climbed inside. Large splashes came in with me. There were several inches of water on the floor and the sump pumps were going full blast. Reaching the control panel, I shut the hatch and opened the ballast tanks, shut the engine and dove to a hundred feet.

My hand opened and closed, so the arm probably wasn't broken but was very sore. It was frightening how close I had come to being washed out to sea. The sub was moving too fast to catch; the shore was too far to swim; the rising storm was overwhelming — not to mention that the water was cold. It was a close call, too close to do anything but shudder. Never again would I be so careless. Never again would I hang out of the portal without some sort of safety line. I would make a harness and attach it to a cable, and wear it whenever the sub was moving, storm or not.

I switched to battery power, reset the sub's course and changed my clothes. The thought of being out in the waves,

fighting for my life, haunted me and I tried to think of other things. But it kept coming back. However I turned it around, the same conclusion loomed in front of me: I would have drowned. I'd be swimming around in the huge waves, going nowhere, swallowing seawater and growing weaker. I might have lasted an hour or so, maybe two. Who knows? But I would have drowned. The sub would have sunk, then come back up. It would have gone until it ran out of gas or hit something. Ziegfried would never know what had happened to me. Neither would anyone else. It would be a short bit on the news — a fourteen-year-old boy lost at sea. Everyone would blame Ziegfried. What a terrible mistake! I had to be so much more careful. The sea didn't care if you were sincere. How true!

After five hours of battery, and two hours of biking, I rose to check on the storm. Even before reaching the surface I could tell it was still raging. It was impossible to walk straight; I had to hold the walls and be careful not to bang my head. Looking out the periscope I couldn't see anything but water. I tried to reach Ziegfried on the short-wave but heard nothing but static. After fifteen minutes of this circus ride, I dove again. How peaceful it was at one hundred feet.

Five hours later I surfaced again. I was out of battery power and had to run the engine. The storm was still raging. I had to hold on to avoid being flung around inside. As much as I wanted to juice up the batteries, it was no fun getting banged up, especially with a sore arm. There was

nothing to do but dive again and pedal. It was becoming clear not only how *dangerous* a storm was, but how *inconvenient* it was. Ten hours of pedalling would only gain one hour of battery power. I was reduced to moving at the speed of a canoe. This was not a comforting thought. What if I had to get out of the way of a supertanker, or, something else?

Murphy's Law. After two and a half hours of pedalling, a beep on the sonar revealed another vessel in the water less than ten miles away. It was coming closer but not directly towards me. If it kept a straight path it would pass by about two miles away. But the closer it came, the more I realized there was something strange about it. Either it was extraordinarily large and deep, or, it was another submarine. If it were a submarine, it had to be a military submarine, which meant it would have listening devices that would tell if it were being detected by another sonar. In other words, they would know I was there.

At six miles I was certain it was a submarine. It was riding between one hundred and fifty and two hundred feet deep. It seemed to take up a lot of space. Then, as I feared, it altered its course and veered slightly in my direction. I didn't know what to do. I couldn't run. If it passed too closely it might spin me around and cause us to collide. If it were a ship, the last thing I would have wanted was to surface. But the sonar clearly indicated it was submerged. I decided to surface.

I came up in the raging storm and frantically scanned the

sea with the periscope. If the sonar were somehow wrong and it *was* a large ship fast approaching, I might get a glimpse of its lights and still have time to dive out of the way. I strained to see in the direction of the sonar beeps but saw nothing. The vessel was closing and would pass on the starboard side. At least it wasn't coming head on.

I decided to dive to fifty feet. That would take me beneath the worst of the storm and maybe offer a peek at the passing sub. I let water into the tanks, went down and stopped tossing like a fish on the wharf. When the approaching vessel was half a mile away and I was confident it would pass by, I went into the bow and sat in the observation window and watched.

Nothing, nothing . . . and then, silently and ghostly, an enormous dark object started to pass below on the starboard side. There seemed no end to it. I even wondered if it had stopped. But the sonar revealed that it was still moving at a steady speed. It was absolutely enormous. The fact that it was so big and could travel so fast beneath the surface, and so quietly, meant it was a nuclear-powered submarine. Most likely it was American. No doubt it had sophisticated devices that told it everything about me. It must have determined that I was no threat because it passed by and continued on its way.

I breathed a sigh of relief. I made a cup of tea, ate two oranges, climbed onto the bike and resumed pedalling. I felt a lot smaller than before.

Chapter Twelve

The storm abated but the sea did not. The rain stopped, the clouds parted and the sun appeared, but the ocean continued to toss like a pot of bubbling soup. I decided to surface anyway and run the risk of getting seasick. It wasn't that I minded pedalling, but I was so far out to sea I couldn't judge if I was getting anywhere. It was possible I was going backwards in the current without even knowing it. So I decided to run the engine and sail within sight of land. At least then I would know.

On the surface I could also call Ziegfried. This time the reception was clear.

"Alfred! I've been trying to reach you for hours! You made it through the storm?"

"It's pretty quiet at a hundred feet."

"You were spotted, Al, by a Norwegian freighter. People have been talking about it on the news. The Coast Guard might send a ship to investigate. Did you see a ship last night?"

"Yes. I saw a submarine too. A really big one."

"Wow! Listen, Al. Don't say too much right now. You know what I mean?"

"Yes."

"It sounds like you're sailing in heavy traffic. Perhaps you should change your strategy?"

"I will. I am."

"Good. How's everything working?"

"Perfect!"

I wanted to tell Ziegfried about getting pulled out in the storm, but didn't want to worry him.

When we finished talking, I heard a noise in the sub. Turning around, I saw something slide down on the floor. Startled, I jumped up and stared at it. It stopped moving. It was green and gray and soaking wet. Coming closer, I realized it was a clump of seaweed. I scratched my head and looked up the portal but saw nothing but open sky. I picked up the seaweed and climbed out. There was no one around.

"That's impossible! A piece of seaweed can't come flying in all by itself!"

I threw it into the water, half expecting some creature to show itself. Perhaps it was a really smart seal that liked to toss things onto rocks. I stared for awhile but never saw anything.

Back inside, I was about to climb onto my seat when something came down the portal again. Turning, I saw the clump of seaweed. I couldn't believe it. I picked it up and looked up the portal, but there was no one.

Someone is playing a trick on me, I thought. But that was impossible; I was miles from anywhere. Climbing the portal, I looked around but there was only water and sky. This time, instead of tossing the seaweed into the sea, I carefully laid it outside the hatch and went back inside. I climbed onto my seat, but kept glancing at the portal, in case the seaweed should reappear.

It did! I couldn't believe it. This time I raced over with the intention of running up the ladder. But when I looked up, I saw a face looking down at me. It had piercing beady eyes and a long curved beak.

"A seagull! Hello!"

The seagull twisted its head and strained to look inside the sub. I picked up the seaweed to give it back but when I looked up again, the gull was gone. I laughed. The mystery was solved.

It was such a rocky ride it was wise not to eat anything. There were seasickness pills if I needed them but I was determined to get my "sea legs." It took about an hour to

come within sight of land, where the sea was calmer. I spent much of that time with my head out the portal and a rope tied around my waist. I was trying to make a friend. I had no idea how a seagull could be so far from land. Perhaps he had been caught in the storm.

I was standing in the portal when a small clump of seaweed hit me on the head. It didn't hurt but it scared the heck out of me. Looking up, I saw the seagull hovering in the sky.

"Wow! You've got really good aim!"

I went inside and brought back a slice of bread and tossed it onto the back of the sub. The seagull promptly landed and gobbled it up. Just five feet away, it looked at me for more. I went inside and returned with another slice. He was waiting. He reached out with his beak, took a few steps closer and stopped.

"It's okay. I won't hurt you."

The seagull tried to claim the bread without coming closer.

"If you want it, you have to take it."

He wanted it very much. He stepped closer and strained his neck as far as possible. Finally, he grabbed one corner and tore it free. He swallowed it in two quick movements, then looked for more.

"Sorry. I have to keep an eye on my rations."

He twisted his head, trying to get a better look at me.

"My name is Alfred. If we are going to be friends, I should

give you a name. Hmmm . . . I think I'll call you . . . 'Seaweed.'"

Seaweed quickly developed the habit of sitting on the hatch whenever it was open. He had the uncanny ability to recognize whenever I was going to eat. If I opened a can of peaches or a box of crackers or peeled an orange, Seaweed would cry out, and I would toss a little bit up the portal, which he would deftly catch and swallow. I had to be careful what I threw in his direction, because he would eat *any-thing*. I also learned that it was the height of rudeness to eat in the presence of a seagull without sharing, as he let me know with really loud squawking — so loud I couldn't eat at all unless I passed some his way.

I had pulled a carrot from the carrot sack and was about to toss up a small bite to Seaweed when there were some beeps on the radar. Coming to the control panel, I was so absorbed in the screen that I forgot all about him, and continued to chew the carrot, without sharing it. The next thing I knew, there was a thump in the sub behind me, and there, standing like a forgotten guest, was Seaweed. He stared all around the inside of the sub as if to say, "This is a weird place."

Then he fixed his beady eyes on me, and the rest of the carrot.

"Oh. Seaweed. I'm sorry. I forgot."

I took one more bite and tossed the remainder to him, who made it disappear in a snap, then promptly climbed

the ladder of the portal as if he were an expert in climbing ladders. I watched with amazement. This was no ordinary seagull.

The beeps on the radar were fishing boats. Likely, they were lobster fishermen coming out to check their traps after the storm. I guessed I was in Deadman's Bay, or thereabouts, but couldn't be sure until I came close enough to identify land features. The closer I drew, the smaller the swells were. A mile from the fishing boats I dove beneath the surface and raised the periscope. What I couldn't know was that Seaweed was riding on top of it.

I passed the boats thinking I was invisible. But the fishermen spotted Seaweed, then the periscope. Word had already spread that a submarine had been seen in the area. The fishermen wasted no time reporting what they saw. Meanwhile, I took refuge in a small cove, dove to seventy-five feet and went to bed. I assumed Seaweed would simply take shelter on shore. I wondered if I would ever see him again.

In the twilight I surfaced and opened the hatch. Seaweed promptly appeared. I greeted him, stretched and yawned. The sea had calmed. I turned on the short-wave and searched for Ziegfried. He wasn't answering. That was strange. Ziegfried had advised me to stay out of the line of ships. It seemed a good idea to hug the coast and look for places to hide in case anyone came searching for me.

Once it was dark I started the engine and sailed out of the cove. Seaweed stood tall on the hatch and pointed out

to sea with his beak. Half a mile out, we turned south and began to follow the coast. Through the periscope I could see lights here and there on the shore — tiny villages, isolated cottages, the occasional island hermit. Ziegfried said not to be surprised to meet strange people in strange places. The sub could sail into the most forbidding passages where even pirates and intrepid sailors couldn't go.

We motored around Cape Freels, and entered Bonavista Bay. We sailed through the night on a wavy sea beneath a clear sky. Seaweed rode the hatch, except when I was eating. Then he scampered inside and squawked for his share of the spoils. I never fed him first because he would only expect more. I saved him the last bite, which he would gobble instantly, then search for more. Once he was convinced there was no more, he would climb the ladder. Gradually, however, he began to linger inside. He was very interested in the radio, especially in certain songs, and especially if I was singing to them while pedalling the bike. Once or twice I caught him swinging his head from side to side with the music.

"Seaweed. You are not a normal seagull. I wonder if you are a bird at all."

Seaweed squawked as if to say, "So? You don't look much like a bird either."

We passed several islands in the night. Then, as we came around one, happily singing and squawking along with the radio, there was a loud beep on the radar. I glanced at the

screen and saw an object coming directly towards us. It was only six miles away. Peering through the periscope, I saw the lights of a ship. I climbed the portal and scanned the sea with the binoculars. Seaweed hopped out and stood on the hull. Straight ahead, we saw the vessel. I was pretty sure it was the coastguard.

"Quick! Seaweed! We've got to dive!"

I made a sweeping gesture with my arm but Seaweed just ignored it.

"Hurry up! Get inside! We have to go!"

He didn't move. Running inside, I opened a can of tuna fish.

"Mmmmmmm . . ." I said.

Seaweed came down the portal in a flash. I flipped the automatic hatch switch, shut the engine and dove to a hundred and fifty feet. The ship closed to four miles. I turned off the radio and sat quietly and shared the tuna fish with Seaweed.

The coastguard vessel came right over us, went a mile past, then turned around. It knew we were there. It came back and passed over us again and continued for two miles in the other direction and stopped. I was anxious to get going but didn't know what to do. I couldn't contact Ziegfried unless we surfaced, and didn't want to do that. The coastguard would detect us as soon as we started to move — by battery for sure, and maybe even by bicycle, I wasn't sure. It would have superior listening devices and might

even know when we were bouncing sonar waves off it. So we sat and waited. Seaweed was good company. I tried to compensate for the lack of radio by singing softly, but he didn't care for it much. He preferred the radio.

The coastguard began to move again. It started a series of passes in a grid-like pattern, but was getting further away each time, which told me they didn't know where we were exactly. When it was nine miles away I decided to run the batteries and see if we could slip away.

It didn't work. Minutes after we started to move, they changed their course and came after us again.

"Rats!"

Suddenly I had an idea. I rose to the surface and started the engine. Seaweed climbed the portal and kept watch on the open hatch. I pointed the bow towards shore and cranked up the engine as fast as it would go. The coastguard pursued us.

"They're chasing us, Seaweed!"

Seaweed squawked.

I gazed at the radar. The coastguard ship was slowly closing the distance between us.

"I don't think she's going a whole lot faster than we are."

I scanned the shore for lights — a fishing village. There was one to our left. I cut the engine, coaxed Seaweed inside, dove to fifty feet, engaged the batteries and turned *right*. On battery power the coastguard would catch us quickly. But we had a nine-mile head start. They could also track us when we were running by battery. And they did. I watched

the sonar as their direction changed to accommodate ours. They were planning to cut us off. As they got closer they would realize we had submerged. I wanted them to think we believed we were escaping. Then, after one mile in that direction, I shut off the batteries, climbed up on the bicycle and turned back towards the fishing village.

The whole strategy was based on the hope they wouldn't detect us if we were moving by bicycle power. I shut the sonar and radio off and tried not to make any loud noises. The bicycle was well greased and quiet. Seaweed settled comfortably on the wooden floor and shut his eyes.

If they knew where we were we would hear their engine at least a mile a way. Stealthily, like a bat under water, I pedalled down the coast, rising ever so gently until the periscope extended above water. When I saw the lights of the little fishing village I turned into the cove. There were seven or eight fishing boats tied to the wharf. I slipped in beneath them and settled to wait for the fishermen to come.

We didn't have to wait long. In little over an hour I heard the coughing of a diesel engine. I could tell it needed a tune up. Ziegfried had taught me well.

A few minutes later another engine started, and then another. I engaged the batteries and got ready to leave. As soon as the boats started to move I followed them. About a mile from shore they cut their engines. We immediately took off. They would begin pulling their traps. The last thing I wanted was to get tangled in lobster traps.

Two miles away I turned on the sonar. Only the seven

fishing boats flashed on the screen. Our escape had been successful. Rising to the surface, I opened the hatch and let Seaweed stretch his wings. I started the engine and headed down the coast. Whoever would have guessed the ocean would be such a busy place?

Chapter Thirteen

There were many islands, large and small, in Bonavista Bay. We passed them as we ran the engine for three hours in the early morning. I kept a close eye on them with the periscope. Ziegfried said there were islanders who kept telescopes pointed out to sea. And many kept short-wave radios, too, and would certainly have heard of the sightings of a submarine and be anxious to see it for themselves. I decided to risk it anyway; our escape from the coastguard gave me confidence in our stealth ability.

Before looking for a place to sleep for the day, I decided to try to reach Ziegfried.

"Alfred! Have you heard? Somebody spotted a submarine in Bonavista Bay. The coastguard is searching for it. They say the navy might too. Isn't that *interesting*?"

"I guess so."

"Nobody knows who it could be. They're afraid it might be a foreign sub . . . you know, a spy sub."

"Oh."

"Anyway, Al. You should give me a *call* sometime, if you ever get to a *phone*. Okay?"

"Oh. Okay. I will."

"Good. Make any friends lately?"

"Um, yes. One."

"Good stuff! *Call* me, okay?"

"I will."

I understood. There were people listening in on the short-wave. Ziegfried didn't want to give anything away. I would have to find a telephone. But where?

On one small rocky island I spotted a sheltered cove. There weren't any cottages in sight.

"Seaweed! Do you want to come inside or stay out while I sleep?"

I looked up the portal and saw Seaweed staring back down.

"Coming in?"

He looked around but didn't answer.

"Well, I'm going to bed."

I flipped the automatic hatch switch. Seaweed hopped

off the hatch and landed on the bow. As the sub descended he flew to a rocky ledge on the island. I caught a glimpse of him with the periscope just before I went under. I went down fifty feet, turned the lights and radio low and went to sleep.

It was dark when I woke and rose to the surface. Having seen no one in the morning, I expected no one at night, and so never bothered to check with the periscope first. To my surprise I was greeted with a bright light. Behind it stood a tall figure in a colourful dress, and, what looked like a whole barnyard of animals. I couldn't see the lady's face but half a dozen dogs, twice as many cats, a goat and bird or two — it was hard to make it out in the dark. Seaweed flew over to the sub as soon as he saw me, and came right to the hatch, so that I could have touched him if I wanted to.

"Hello there!" called the lady. "Creature from the deep."

"Hello."

"Are you from Atlantis?"

"No. Newfoundland."

"You don't look like a Newfoundlander to me."

Neither do you, I thought, but didn't say that out loud.

"Are you by yourself?"

"Yes. Well . . . except for him."

I nodded towards Seaweed.

"All creatures of the sea are welcome here. Would you like to come in for tea?"

I hesitated. I looked around to see if anyone else was there.

"We live alone here. My friends and me."

I noticed she called her pets "friends," just as Ziegfried did.

"Um . . . I guess I could."

"Wonderful! It has been so long since we had a creature from the sea come in for tea."

I wondered who the last guest was.

I jumped to the rock and tied up the sub carefully to keep it from banging against the rocks. Seaweed stayed on the hatch; he wasn't fussy about the dogs and cats. The dogs *were* fussy about me. They sniffed me from head to toe and made it impossible to walk.

"Ladies!" said the lady with the light, "give our guest some room, please!"

I followed her up the path to her cottage, built right into the rock. It was sheltered on three sides and open on one to the sea and sunrise.

"My name is Sheba. Like the queen. Welcome."

"Thank you. My name is Alfred."

"Like the king."

"There was a King Alfred?"

"Alfred the Great! King of the Saxons. What kind of tea would you like?"

She smiled. She was tall, like Ziegfried. She had long, red hair that streamed down her back and shoulders in chains of little curls. Her face was bright and shiny. She had wide,

green eyes and a large, red mouth. Every time she spoke she looked directly into my eyes. Her eyes twinkled. I liked her very much.

"Isn't there only one kind of tea?"

"Only one kind of tea?"

She examined me as if I were a fish she had pulled from the sea.

"Isn't tea just tea?"

"Oh my stars no. There are as many kinds of tea as there are shades of green. Do you know how many shades of green there are?"

"No."

"Thousands."

"Oh."

"I'll tell you what: I'll choose a tea for you and you see if you like it. Okay?"

"Okay."

I followed her into her kitchen. There were hanging pots and pans, bottles and jars, with powders and spices and every sort of thing. There were dried flowers and herbs hanging from the rafters and potted plants with tomatoes and peppers growing beneath bright lights. There were urns and bowls and vases, and some of the vases were filled with dried flowers and some with fresh. It was an indoor garden. Everything was bright and colourful.

"I will make you some . . . red bush tea . . . with vanilla, from South Africa."

She poured water into the kettle, opened the stove and

tossed in three pieces of driftwood.

"Have you been to South Africa?" I asked.

She looked up. Her lovely smile was replaced with a sad one.

"Yes. I have been everywhere."

She scooped flecks of tea into a metal ball, dangling from a chain, and dropped it into a teapot that looked like Aladdin's lamp. As I watched her hands move I thought of Ziegfried.

"And you? Have you been everywhere in that sea craft of yours?"

"Nope. But I'm planning to go everywhere. I just started."

She grinned.

"I thought you were a monster. We came down to the rock and saw something under the water. But you didn't move."

"I was sleeping."

She clapped her hands and laughed.

"Sleeping? Down there in the deep cold?"

"It's not so deep. And not so cold."

"For a *fish*."

"How come you . . . I mean, how did you travel to so many places?"

She sighed.

"My mother was a famous opera singer. We travelled everywhere when I was little."

"Didn't you go to school?"

"No. I taught myself mostly. I read a lot. When you travel, you learn, as you will see."

"Did your father travel with you?"

She turned to the stove and poured water into the teapot.

"I never saw my father a lot. But I loved him very much."

She sat at the table. Even though she was smiling, tiny tears appeared on the bottoms of her eyes.

"Once, when I was twelve, my father came to see me. We were staying in a villa in the south of France, where my mother was preparing for a new opera season. He took me for rides in his car and told me how much he loved me. Then he gave me the most beautiful necklace."

Sheba's eyes welled up with tears. I didn't know what to do.

"I'm sorry," she said.

"That's okay."

"It was the last time I saw him. But I kept that necklace. It was my favourite. It had a silver chain with gold and silver pendants — stars and the sun and moon. Oh, how I loved it."

"What happened to it?"

"I lost it when I came here."

"How?"

"A mermaid took it."

"A *mermaid*?"

"Yes."

"You believe in mermaids?"

"Of course."

"Oh. Why . . . um . . . why do you think a mermaid took it?"

"Mermaids are jealous of beautiful things, especially jewelry. I should have known better. I left my necklace on the rock, where your submarine is, when I took my clothes off to go swimming. When I came out of the water, it was gone. But my clothes were still there."

"But how do you know it was a mermaid? Did you see it?"

"No, but I had a very strong feeling that a mermaid had just been there. I could smell her."

"What do mermaids smell like?"

"Like the ocean, and . . . exotic spices."

"Have you ever *seen* a mermaid?"

"Not up close, but from a distance. And you often hear them at night."

"What do they sound like?"

"They have strange singing voices, not like humans at all. It's a kind of high-pitched wailing. Very mysterious and not really beautiful."

"Oh."

I took a drink of tea.

"How is your tea?"

"Delicious. But it tastes like . . . cake."

Sheba laughed. Her face brightened again and filled the whole kitchen. Her dogs and cats were smiling too. I once

read a story about sailors who were turned into animals by a beautiful woman. I scanned my tea for a magic potion. Something about Sheba made me feel anything was possible.

We stayed up most of the night. Over five cups of tea I learned that Sheba believed in pretty much everything. She said she regularly saw ghosts — sailors mostly, and that there was a very good spot on the island for watching the ghost ship of Bonavista Bay, that I would certainly see it if I stayed around long enough. She spoke so convincingly about these things that after a few hours, and some very strange but delicious tea, I didn't know *what* to believe anymore. I did want to consider the existence of things not yet seen. Did that include ghosts and mermaids?

Chapter Fourteen

When I returned to the sub, the sky was almost blue. But I wasn't sleepy. There was something I wanted to do. Sheba said she lost her necklace right off the rock, and I wanted to see if I could find it, mermaid or not.

The sonar revealed a bottom of eighty-five feet, with several deeper pockets, like a huge honeycomb. I couldn't bring the sub to the bottom but had to hover over each pocket and peer into it from the observation window. My guess was that Sheba's necklace had fallen off the rock somehow. As Seaweed crowded into the observation window with me I thought of something else.

"Maybe a seagull took it!"

Seaweed squawked at that idea. Maybe a crab crawled onto the rock, picked up the necklace and pulled it over the side. The cove was narrow, sheltered and dark below the surface so I could understand why Sheba thought it was much deeper than it was.

Shutting the hatch, I dove to seventy-five feet and hit the outside lights. There was no point waiting for the sun; it wouldn't help down there. The lights were bright enough but I couldn't move them; I had to move the whole sub, which was difficult in such a small cove. All I could really do was spin it around in circles by turning the rudder sharply and pedalling on the bike. Seaweed found my interest in the observation window compelling, and stared down every time I did. Once in a while he pecked at the glass.

It was very tedious. All of the pockets looked the same — sand and a few rocks and clumps of seaweed. Here and there were lines under the sand that could have been anything — a necklace or a piece of rope. But there were too many. In one pocket was a lobster trap, and dangling on one side was something kind of shiny, though it could have been light reflecting off a piece of rope or seaweed or anything. Try as I might, I couldn't make it out. But Seaweed started to peck at it through the glass. Then it occurred to me: seagulls have excellent vision. He could see whatever it was much better than I could, and he was *pecking* at it.

The problem was, it was sitting at eighty-five feet, and

the water was pretty cold, and once I brought the sub to the surface, the pockets would be in darkness again. Well . . . I *did* have an underwater flashlight and I *did* have a wetsuit. But eighty-five feet was ten feet deeper than my maximum diving depth. On the other hand . . . what I wouldn't give to bring Sheba's precious necklace back.

We rose to the surface, opened the hatch and Seaweed hopped out. I dug out the wet suit and flashlight. After a few minutes of swimming around the sub, which Seaweed found so intriguing he had to join me, I started preparations for diving. I took long, deep breaths and visualized myself going down with ease and calmly sifting through the sand at the bottom. Then I visualized rising to the surface with the necklace in my hand. All of this was relaxed and comfortable.

Well, that was a nice visualization. The truth was, I couldn't seem to get warm or comfortable enough. On the first dive it was probably sixty-five feet when I felt anxiety for the pressure and darkness, and eighty-five feet seemed unreachable. Sheba's stories of mermaids and ghosts kept jumping into my head.

The second dive was better. I think I reached seventy-five feet. The pressure was heavier but I had less anxiety. On the third dive I touched the top of one of the pockets, about eighty feet down — my deepest dive ever. But it wasn't the one with the lobster trap. On the fourth dive I spotted the trap, touched the top of the pocket and turned around. I

was only six feet from the trap, but somehow, swimming into the pocket was like swimming into a cave, and I was spooked.

Back on the surface I felt frustrated.

"Just do it! Stop turning around and wasting time!"

On the fifth dive I reached the top of the pocket again, touched the rock and pulled myself down towards the trap. I pointed the flashlight. There it was, covered with sea growth and sand — Sheba's beloved necklace!

One touch of the chain shook the sand free but the chain was wound around the edge of the trap and I needed more time to free it. My head ached with sharp pain on the way up but cleared at the top. Eighty-five feet was too deep for me, but I wanted that necklace.

On the sixth dive I finally got it. I also picked up a head-ache that lingered for awhile. But I was happy, especially for Sheba. She was in for a surprise.

Back in the sub I rinsed the necklace in fresh water and picked debris from it. It was tarnished but I knew she could clean and polish it. I felt like rushing right over but decided to sleep first. Seaweed had spotted a flock of seagulls and took off to join them. I watched him rise in wide circles until he was way above, and then I couldn't tell which one was him. I shut the hatch and went down fifty feet, had a bowl of cereal and an orange before bed. But something was nagging me. I decided to call Ziegfried. So I resurfaced and turned on the short-wave.

"Al! How's it going, Buddy?"

"Good. Do you believe in mermaids?"

"Mermaids? Good Heavens! Have you seen mermaids?"

"No. But . . . do you believe in them?"

"Well, I can't say that I do; I've never seen one."

"What about ghosts?"

"Oh yes, I do believe in ghosts."

"You *do*?"

"Yup."

"Oh."

"Why do you ask, have you seen one?"

"No, but I've met somebody who has."

"Interesting. So, Al. Are you riding your bike a lot these days? I hope so. That's a great way to get around, eh?"

"Yes. I think so too. I'm planning to ride quite a bit."

"Very good. And don't forget to call as soon as you find a phone, okay?"

"Okay. But I haven't seen too many phones yet."

Ziegfried laughed.

"No, I don't imagine."

After talking with Ziegfried I went back down to fifty feet, turned the lights down and climbed into bed. But it was hard to sleep thinking of Sheba's necklace and Ziegfried believing in ghosts. That was hard to understand. Back and forth between Sheba and Ziegfried my mind wandered until sleep took hold of it. It was still kind of fuzzy when I woke and rose in the twilight. But there was Sheba, waiting

with her animals. I opened the hatch and Seaweed suddenly appeared.

"Alfred! Dear friend!" called Sheba. "Won't you please come over for tea?"

I couldn't help but grin from ear to ear. I gave Seaweed two cookies and hopped onto the rock and tied up. Sheba's dogs jumped all over me, full of joy. Sheba was wearing a purple dress with beads that clinked together when she moved. She smiled in her wonderful, magical way.

"I have something for you," I said, and reached into my pocket.

"You have something for *me*? What could that be?"

"Something I found."

"Something you found? Where did you find it?"

"In the sea."

"In the sea . . ."

I pulled the necklace out and handed it to her. She put her hand to her mouth and cried, "Oooooooooh!"

Her eyes filled with tears as she took the necklace from my hand. She stared at it in her own hands and started sobbing. I didn't know what to do. I guessed she was happy but she was crying so much it was hard to tell. Finally, she looked up, took a deep breath, grabbed my hand and said, "Where did you find it?"

"There."

I pointed beside the sub.

"But how?"

"I dove for it."

"With your sea-craft?"

"No, free-dive."

She looked confused.

"You *swam* down there?"

I nodded.

"It's not *so* far. Well, it *was* pretty far but I have a lot of practice diving. That was the deepest I ever went. Eighty-five feet."

"Oh, Alfred. I will be forever grateful to you. I cannot believe I have it back. Do you know what this means to me? This is the most important thing I have."

"I know. You told me. I'm really happy you have it back."

She held her heart and took deep breaths.

"Oh. I can't believe it. I am so happy. Thank you, Alfred. Thank you *so much*."

She began to cry again. Then she came over and hugged me.

"You're welcome," I said.

After a second night in Sheba's kitchen I was anxious to return to sea. Her stories of strange places and things only filled me with more desire to explore and I could hardly sit still. One story in particular was luring me out: the Flaming Ghost Ship of Bonavista Bay. In ten years, Sheba had seen the ship dozens of times. She said all we had to do was stay up all night and stare out at sea. The fall was the best time.

Well, staying up all night was my regular sailing time. But sitting on a rock, waiting for a ghost ship to appear was not my style; I wanted to get out and search for it, if such a thing did exist. I had my doubts.

But I was about to find out.

Chapter Fifteen

The fog curled thick around us the night we left Sheba's cove. She came down to the water to see us off with presents: crackers for Seaweed and tea for me. I promised to visit again. As we glided away from the rocks I glanced through the periscope and saw her glowing with light, surrounded by the dark outline of her animals.

The open sea never regained any semblance of calm. On the mainland side of an island it settled down a bit, and we could enjoy sitting in the open portal, the harness snug around my waist. But the open sea always looked like a storm waiting to happen. Of course, beneath the surface, all

was calm. But the practical truth of the sub's capabilities became increasingly clear: if we wanted to poke around islands and coves we could do just fine submerged; if we ever wanted to cross any distance, we had to travel on the surface.

We spun around Sheba's island and went straight out to sea. I wanted to get back into the lane of traffic where Sheba said she had seen the ghost ship. I kept a close eye on the radar and periscope. It was a quiet night. At one point Seaweed broke the silence with loud squawking on the starboard side. I turned a floodlight towards the water and scanned the waves but saw nothing. Seaweed was a pretty reliable scout though, so there must have been something there; I just couldn't see it.

After an uneventful night of cruising southward, about five miles from shore, I decided to seek another sheltered cove before the sun came up. It was only after we changed course that we heard a beep on the radar. I definitely heard it, but when I glanced at the panel, there was nothing.

That's strange, I thought, is there something, or not?

Seaweed twisted his head.

"Maybe I only thought I heard it. Maybe I heard something else."

Then, there it was again. This time I saw the light blink on the screen. No doubt about it. But it only blinked once.

That was very strange! I needed to see it beep just once more to know if it were coming or going. So I sat and stared

at the screen for a long time, but nothing happened.

"Maybe there's something in the periscope."

I took a careful 360-degree look.

"Nope. Nothing."

The radar beeped again. I dashed over but didn't get there in time to see it.

"Rats!"

Now I didn't know what to do. Should I go searching for it, or find a cove for the day?

"What should we do, Seaweed?"

Seaweed tapped his beak on the screen.

"Okay. We'll take one quick look, then head for cover."

We spun around 180 degrees and headed north. I climbed the portal and scanned the horizon. The fog was clearing and there was a thin dark blue line in the east. Suddenly there was brilliant light, just like the rising sun.

That can't be the sun, I thought, it's too early. I stared hard at the flashing light, which, from a distance, did look like flames.

"What is it, Seaweed?"

In the pre-dawn the flaming light on the horizon was beautiful, not spooky at all. Is this what Sheba had seen? Then, the flames were gone. I stared for another twenty minutes, while the blue spread across the sky. The real sun would soon be up.

"Well, Seaweed, we'd better head in."

I went inside and changed course again. Seaweed stayed

up on the portal and watched the sunrise. A few minutes later there was a beep on the radar. It was only five miles away. I raced to the periscope. Nothing. The radar beeped again. The object was now four miles away.

"That's not possible. Nothing can move that fast, except an airplane, and I don't hear one."

The radar beeped again. Three miles and coming directly towards us.

"That's crazy! There's nothing there!"

On the next beep the object was only two miles away. I felt a sudden panic. Maybe something was going to collide with us. Should I try to dive? There was hardly time to do anything. I breathed deeply, then rushed up the portal and stared hard in the direction of the beeps. I could see clearly; there was nothing there. I rushed back inside. Could it be coming underwater? I stared at the sonar. Nothing. The radar beeped once more. One mile away! I rushed up the portal again and stared as hard as I could. Nothing. Whatever was coming would be upon us in an instant. I braced myself, half expecting an impact.

But nothing came. *Now* I was spooked. Were there ghosts around us? It didn't feel like it. What were ghosts supposed to feel like anyway?

Half an hour later we motored into the bay and found a cove in one of the outer islands. Seaweed stayed up. I wondered if he would sleep on land because he didn't sleep much at night. He had become nocturnal, like me. Before

sleep I caught up in my captain's log, describing the night as faithfully as possible — for Ziegfried's Christmas reading. Was it a ghost encounter? I didn't think so, but I could understand why other people would.

The following night I decided to moor close enough to Bonavista to walk into town in the morning and find a telephone. Cape Bonavista, with its bright lighthouse, was easy to spot. But the town didn't have much of a harbour and it was difficult to find a cove to hide the sub. Back and forth I scanned the coast with the periscope before choosing a spot close to town. Seaweed stayed with the sub as I climbed a hill, passed through a woods and stepped onto the road.

I had no idea which day of the week it was. No one was around. Maybe it was Sunday. Then I saw a school bus. Eventually I saw a church, some stores, a bowling alley, and . . . a telephone booth. I put a quarter in, called the operator, and was connected to Ziegfried.

"Al! Where on earth are you?"

"Bonavista."

"Bonavista! Where did you tie up?"

"A few miles from town. I had to walk."

"How's the sub?"

"Perfect. I have a crew."

"A crew?"

"A seagull."

"Hah!"

"His name is Seaweed. You would like him; he's got a great eye for things and is good company."

Ziegfried laughed.

"I met a wonderful lady too."

"You met a lady? Where would you meet a lady? Al . . . don't tell me she's a mermaid?"

"No. At least I don't think so. Did you ever hear of the Ghost Ship of Bonavista Bay?"

"Oh yes. I know people who have seen her. Have you seen her, Al?"

"I don't know. I saw *something*. It followed us on the radar, then there was nothing."

"Al. You said, 'us.' Who's 'us'?"

"Seaweed and me."

"The seagull?"

"Yes."

"Listen, Al. The coastguard is searching for you. If they think you're a threat, they'll bring in the navy. If the navy thinks you're a spy sub they won't think twice about firing at you. The first shot would be a warning shot, Al. And Heavens Alive, if they ever do that, surface right away and raise a white flag. They've got such sophisticated missile systems they could hit you on the nose from a hundred miles away."

"Well, they can't hear me when I'm just pedalling. I already escaped from the coastguard once."

"Gosh, Al, I thought you might have to run from pirates

someday; I never thought you'd be running from the authorities."

He paused.

"That makes you an outlaw."

"Don't worry about me; the sub is really small and can hide anywhere. They'll never catch me."

"I hope not. And if they do, perhaps they'll realize you're not a threat and will just let you go."

"They have to catch me first. By the way . . . that lady's name is Sheba, and she is really nice, and, she keeps birds."

"*Does* she now?"

"She's really interesting."

"*Is* she now?"

"Yup."

I started laughing.

"Well, that's good, Al. Keep your eyes on the horizon now."

"Will do."

After talking with Ziegfried I went into a store to buy some pop and candy — things I didn't have on the sub. I swung open the door, and there, standing at the counter, were two sailors from the coastguard! I was startled but quickly realized there was no way they could know who I was. As I went to the back of the store for pop I heard them talking with the clerk.

"So you think maybe it's a Russian sub, do you?" said the clerk.

"Who knows? Whoever it is, they're pretty shrewd. They gave us the slip twice. But we'll catch them. The navy's got a tight radar net ten miles off shore. We'll catch them when they try to get through that."

The second sailor nudged the first one.

"Joe. You're not supposed to say anything to anybody, you know that."

"Oh, who's he gonna tell? Don't tell anybody I told you that, okay, buddy? I didn't say anything."

The clerk shrugged his shoulders.

"Don't worry; I didn't hear anything. You don't suppose that sub's carrying nuclear missiles, do you?"

"No, no. It's just a tiny thing. It's one of those mini-subs, you know, that sneak into harbours to spy on naval bases and such."

"Joe, will you shut up? We're not supposed to say anything."

"Oh yah. Sorry. Listen. Don't repeat anything I told you. I didn't say anything."

"Don't worry, I won't breathe a word."

When the sailors left the store I went up to the cash.

"Were those guys with the coastguard?" I asked innocently.

"Yah. They're chasing that Russian sub."

"What Russian sub?"

"The sub that everybody's talking about. The sub that's spying on us. Haven't you heard? Where're you from anyway, I haven't seen you here before?"

"I'm from the country. I'm just visiting here for the day. Do you know where the coastguard ship is, I'd love to get a look at it?"

"It's up at the lighthouse. But don't tell anybody I told you; they're trying to be really secret about it."

"Okay, I won't. Which way is the lighthouse?"

"Just take that road there. Or, follow those two sailors who just left."

I did exactly that. Before long, I caught up to them. I couldn't resist the opportunity to talk to my pursuers.

"Hey, are you guys with the coastguard?"

"We sure are. What's *your* name?"

"Alfred."

"Hello, Alfred. My name is Joe, and this is Eddie."

"How are ya?" said Eddie.

"Fine," I said. "Where's your ship?"

"Just off the point," said Joe. "We're keeping a close eye out for that submarine."

"Oh yah. I heard about it. Do you think it's dangerous?"

"Well, you never know. If it's spying on us it can't be up to any good. But don't you worry about it; we're gonna catch that thing any time now."

I nodded and chewed my candy.

"Hey, could I look at your ship? I've never seen a coast-guard ship up close."

That, at least, was the truth.

"Sure you can. Just come up to the lighthouse and you'll

see her. Are you thinking of joining the coastguard some-day?"

"I don't know."

"It's a good life," said Joe, "if you like the water."

Joe and Eddie were so friendly I wished I could have told them I was the submariner. I even wondered if Joe might have kept it a secret. Then I thought: nope, probably not.

"So . . . what will you do with the spies when you catch them?"

"Oh . . . the navy will put them in jail; interrogate them. They'll be put on trial, and probably locked away in some prison somewhere for fifty years."

I didn't like the sound of that.

"But . . . what if it's just somebody local, somebody who built their own submarine?"

Joe and Eddie burst out laughing.

"Well . . ." said Joe, "in the first place, nobody's got that kind of technology, except the navy, and us."

"The coastguard doesn't have submarines, Joe," said Eddie.

"Well . . . the navy. And secondly, even if they did, they'd never be able to outsmart the coastguard and the navy. Nope. This submarine might be clever, but we've got a radar net, and tomorrow the Sea Kings are coming. That will put an end to it for sure. Look. There's our ship."

The road came to an end at the lighthouse. Down below, in the water, sat the bright red and white coastguard ship. A

tinge of nervousness struck me when I saw it.

"Sorry, Alfred," said Joe. "If it were any other time we'd invite you down to visit the ship but right now we're on high alert and visitors are not allowed."

"That's okay. I'm just glad to see it."

I was about to say, "I hope you catch that sub," but couldn't quite get the words out. Joe and Eddie waved as they went down the hill. At the last second I had a thought.

"Hey! When do you sail?"

"Tonight!" yelled Joe.

I saw Eddie nudge Joe again.

Chapter Sixteen

The coastguard slipped away in the night, but didn't go far. I watched through the periscope as she went out gently, just a few miles offshore. I knew she was listening in all directions with every device on board, playing her part in the radar net. I could only hope that, as before, she couldn't detect us on bicycle power. My plan was to pedal around the cape and sneak down the coast. But the presence of Sea Kings would make that a lot more difficult. Sea Kings were helicopters that could spot anything in the water in the daytime. No doubt they would fly up and down the shore, checking every cove and harbour. My daytime hiding places would have to be a lot more secretive.

It was a long night of pedalling. Seaweed kept me company but the nighttime had finally caught up to him and he found a cozy spot on the floor and went to sleep. I listened to the radio. The news said there were reports of an unidentified submarine off the coast of Newfoundland. The navy wouldn't comment on whether or not they were investigating. I couldn't believe it; we had made the national news. We were famous . . . sort of. But all I really wanted was to be free to explore. If we could just escape this net.

By morning we rounded the cape into the mouth of Trinity Bay. Now we faced a difficult choice. Straight across the Bay was about twenty nautical miles, which we could sail by engine in about two hours. But it was open water all the way. The other option — to hug the coast — would take us all the way in and around Trinity Bay, which, by a combination of pedalling, battery and engine power, would take at least four to five days. What to do? I decided to sleep on it and started searching for underwater formations to hide us from the sky. Then something occurred to me. Joe and Eddie said the coastguard and navy were watching their radar at night, and that the Sea Kings would be out in the day, scanning the coastline like hawks. What if I sailed straight across the mouth of the bay, on the surface, right in the middle of day — the last thing anybody would expect? It seemed pretty risky, and yet, perhaps the best strategy was the one nobody would think of. I remembered what Joe had said — nobody could outsmart the navy and coastguard. The truth was — that was my best chance.

A little offshore I dove to two hundred feet and sat on the bottom. I decided to sleep first and cross the bay in the late afternoon. That would give the Sea Kings time to arrive. My biggest fear was to run into them on our way across.

Seaweed took to the sky as I went down. I hoped he would be there when I came back up. Eight hours later, he was. With the hatch wide open and the engine cranked as high as it would go, we set off across the bay. I sat down with a cup of hot chocolate and watched the screens, once in a while climbing the portal to join Seaweed in searching the sky.

All was quiet until about halfway across when the radar beeped. There was a vessel sailing in the other direction about eight miles away. I looked through the binoculars. Probably it was a freighter. It never changed its course. It would have known we were there but would not have been able to see us. Would that make it suspicious? Perhaps. A little further on there was another beep in the same lane of traffic. Maybe they were sister ships. They might have been navy ships, but they never changed their course.

Soon I spotted land. I wanted to get as close as I dared, then dive and finish by pedal. There was barely half an hour left; then, just twenty-five minutes; then twenty; then . . . another beep on the radar. It was ten miles behind us. Suddenly it was nine miles and closing.

"A Sea King! Quick! Seaweed! Get inside! We have to dive!"

In a panic I grabbed a bag of raisins and shook it. Seaweed

started down the portal. I shut the engine, sealed the hatch, filled the tanks and dove as quickly as possible. I took a quick glance at the ocean depth before shutting off the sonar and dove to two hundred and fifty feet. It was the deepest the sub had ever gone. Seaweed quickly pecked at the raisins, then squawked for more.

"Quiet, Seaweed. We have to be very quiet."

Without radar or periscope I had no idea what was happening on the surface or in the sky. There was no way to know if the Sea King had seen us or not but I was pretty sure they couldn't see us now.

"Seaweed, we have to wait until dark."

He seemed kind of restless so I played with him. I tossed him raisins, one at a time. I threw them high or low or off to one side. He jumped at them like a dog catching a ball.

When I knew it was dark I started pedalling. It would take at least two hours to pedal in. At two hundred and fifty feet we would strike the bottom long before we reached the shore so I frequently jumped off the bike, scurried over to the observation window and stared down with the floodlights. A Sea King would have powerful floodlights too, but would have to know pretty much where we were coming up to be able to catch us in their light. I was more concerned they would drop a cable with sonar, or that they had placed another ship in the area already.

An hour from shore I caught a glimpse of the ocean floor. Actually, Seaweed saw it first and pecked at the window.

Now the tricky thing was to come in without radar or sonar. We had to surface and watch through the periscope for ships or rocky promontories. And there was no light, except for the blinking lights on shore, which guided us in. My plan was as before: find a cove, sneak in beneath a fishing boat and hide.

We rose gingerly and I opened the hatch and let Seaweed out. Nothing showed through the periscope but shore lights so I climbed the portal and took a good look. Clusters of lights blinked here and there on the water, which meant a dock or a few moored sailboats. As I pedalled closer, I discovered the lights were coming from a tugboat hooked to a barge of scrap metal. No doubt the tugboat was going to pull the barge to St. John's for recycling. Suddenly I got a wonderful idea.

Keeping clear of the tugboat, I pedalled in an arc and came up behind the barge. I dropped a line into the water to determine the depth. Seventy-five feet. That meant there was plenty of room underneath. Barges were wide but not very deep. The only thing I didn't know was when it was leaving.

Under shelter of night I moored the sub to the back of the barge, then climbed on to have a look around. It was like a floating junkyard. There were lots of pipe, iron girders, aluminum rails, steel rods, empty tanks and wheels. The metal was packed tightly and it amazed me the barge could even float.

I went to the front cautiously and peeked at the tugboat. There didn't seem to be anyone around. There were a few dim safety lights here and there but the cabin was in darkness. The tugboat was connected to the barge by a heavy chain that disappeared beneath the water between them.

And so, sitting on the ocean side of the barge, my feet dangling over the side, feeling restless, I proceeded to do one of the dumbest things I've ever done. I pulled a pack of matches from my pocket, lit one and dropped it into the water. The match made a fiery plunge to the ocean. I imagined it a WWI airplane falling from the skies. I lit another and watched it burn a brilliant streak all the way down to the water. It was kind of hypnotic. I lit several more and watched them burn brightly before disappearing into blackness. But one of the matches ignited too close to my fingers and I threw it sideways to avoid getting burnt. The match landed on the floor of the barge, where, in a mixture of gas and oil, it spread into a larger flame. I stared with amazement as the flame grew. Jumping to my feet, I stepped on it, trying to snuff it out, but the flame was floating on a pool of spilled fuel. Suddenly it roared up to my height and I had to back away. I couldn't stop it. For a few seconds I stared in disbelief. Then I realized — *this* would be seen from shore.

I looked around for a pail or something to hold water. But the water was too far to reach anyway, unless I jumped in, and then I wouldn't be able to reach the top of the barge again. I looked at shore. Surely people would see the fire

and come out to investigate. Then they would see the sub. What should I do? What should I do? All my life I'd heard people say, "Don't play with matches!" Now I knew why.

If the fire continued to spread, I knew it might cause an explosion. I stared hard at shore. Did a light just go on? Yes. Someone had started up a boat and was coming out. I jumped onto the sub and unhooked it from the barge. A floodlight scanned over the water. I jumped inside, shut the hatch and went down to periscope level. Sure enough, two boats were racing out. I dove to fifty feet and sat quietly and listened.

In a few minutes I heard the motors of two small boats. I flipped the sonar switch. It revealed the barge and tugboat, two small boats at the scene and two more on their way out, nothing else. I engaged the batteries, went a mile straight out and surfaced. From that distance the fire on the barge was tiny. Thank Heavens there was no explosion. Still, I felt terrible. I might have blown the whole thing sky high.

With several boats in the area I took the chance to switch on the radar. It was clear within a ten-mile radius. I turned on the radio. They said a big storm was coming. All ocean-craft were advised to take cover. That was funny; there weren't any signs of a storm. I looked around for Seaweed, but he was nowhere to be seen. It was a good time to leave, but I couldn't go without my crew. And so, I opened a can of beans for supper, got comfortable in the portal and watched the fire burn. It burned for most of the night. They

must have decided to let it burn itself out without spreading.

For hours I watched the barge and the boats around it, until a thin line of red appeared on the horizon and I remembered the old saying:

Red sky at night, sailors' delight;
Red sky at morning, sailors take warning.

Well, if they were predicting a storm, the sky seemed to agree. Now I had to go, or at least dive. But where was Seaweed? I waited as long as possible, then went just beneath the waves, leaving the periscope up. Maybe, with his amazing vision, he would see the periscope from shore. I climbed onto the bicycle and started to pedal. But the morning was my bedtime and sleep was catching up with me. If only there were a place hidden from the Sea Kings, where I could steal some sleep, then look for Seaweed again just before dark. A couple of miles out, the ocean floor went down to one hundred and fifty feet. I engaged the batteries, went out and dove to the bottom, put the lights low and drifted off to a peaceful sleep.

It was peaceful waking, too. But that was at a hundred and fifty feet. Rising to the surface I discovered that the storm had rolled in during the day. It wasn't raining yet but the wind was very strong and the swells were high. This was the kind of weather where you wanted to stay indoors, or,

on the ocean floor. On the other hand, this was a great opportunity to sail out of the area altogether since the coastguard and navy would not be on the go, nor would the Sea Kings be in the air. I had an important objective first, of course — to find Seaweed.

There wasn't much time. Twilight had settled early. I was three miles offshore and visibility wasn't good. Turning on all systems I sailed full speed towards the barge. Half a mile away I stopped — hoping the tossing waves would hide the sub from shore. I stood up on the portal with the harness and scanned the sky for any sign of my friend. Around the barge was a flock of birds struggling in the wind. Was Seaweed amongst them?

Before long, one of the birds separated from the others, rose high into the air and began to fight his way in my direction. It must have been Seaweed. He had spotted me.

"Come on, Seaweed!" I yelled. "You can make it!"

It wasn't easy for him. The wind tossed him around like a sheet of paper, and sometimes threatened to knock him into the sea. But gradually, with a determination that really impressed me, he came closer. Suddenly the rain started and came down hard. It became much more difficult to see. One moment I could see Seaweed; the next I couldn't. I was afraid he might get injured trying to land on the sub in such high winds. I needn't have worried; he was too smart for that. Coming out of the sky in a desperate lunge he made a crash landing away from the sub, then merely paddled the

rest of the way. When he was close, he took to the air again. I ducked inside and he followed immediately after. Inside, he shook the beads of water from his head and shook his feathers out. I promptly offered him two slices of bread, which he gobbled in a flash, then blinked as if to say thank you.

"Glad you made it, Seaweed."

I shut the hatch and we headed out to sea.

Chapter Seventeen

Until you have witnessed a storm at sea, you can't imagine how violent it can be. Giant waves throw you up in the air like a leaf, then hurl you down and crush you beneath tons of water. They spin you around and around like a washing machine, and cover you in an attempt to drown you. Sometimes they simply smash against you like a wall of bricks. Not for a second can you find any peace.

We dove to one hundred feet and switched to battery power. We weren't far from Grates Cove and the mouth of Conception Bay. I figured if we could get across the bay during the storm we'd be pretty much home free. St. John's

wasn't far from the other side, and, with all the sea traffic in and out of the capital city we would be next to invisible. I had never been to St. John's before but Ziegfried said you could find really good pizza there.

With the radio on and Seaweed cozy in the observation window, I climbed onto the bike and started to pedal. We had ten hours of battery power. I intended to increase it to eleven by pedalling through the night. And then, I heard something on the radio that disturbed me.

Along with warnings for fishermen and sailors to stay off the water, the radio said that the coastguard had received a Mayday from a sailboat caught in the storm, but that they had to wait until the storm lessened before attempting a rescue. As I pedalled the bike I couldn't help thinking that somewhere out in the storm, perhaps not so far from me, was a family in deep trouble. They were signalling for help but nobody was coming. The more I thought about it, the more upsetting it was. I remembered being swept over the side of the sub in the last storm and how frightening that was. But this was worse. Was there anything I could do?

I decided to surface and turn on the short-wave. Maybe somebody would know something. Maybe I could reach Ziegfried and ask his advice. Coming up, I could feel the storm had become even worse. Nothing came through the short-wave but static. I flipped through the channels, hearing bits of sound, different languages, but nothing understandable. I scanned the radar. Nothing. The storm was

tossing us around so much I had to hold on tightly. Seaweed kept shifting his weight from foot to foot. He wasn't too happy about the storm either.

"I know, I know," I said, "we should go back down where it's quiet."

But the thought that there were people out there, desperately hoping and praying that someone would hear them and save them, kept me from diving. I decided to try the short-wave again. I went around and around the channels. And then I heard it: a man's voice. He sounded desperate.

"... please help ... north ... northwest ..."

He said some numbers but I couldn't make them out. There was too much static. He said it again.

"... S.O.S. ... distress ... help ... northwest ..."

I got part of the coordinates that time, looked at my map and tried to figure out where they could be. The area was too wide; they could have been anywhere. I tried reaching them on the short-wave.

"What ... are ... your ... coordinates?"

There was a pause, and then his voice again, more frantic. This time I got it. I stared at the map. They were at least twenty-five to thirty nautical miles away. In such a storm, that might as well have been a hundred. But I made a decision then that I would do absolutely everything I could to try to help them.

"Hold on!" I said. "I am coming!"

"... how long? ..." I heard him say.

I thought about it. Three or four hours might have been realistic, I didn't know for sure, but I wanted to give them hope. Something told me they needed hope as much as anything else.

"Two hours!" I yelled. "Hold on!"

I opened the medicine cabinet and took some seasickness pills, then opened the hatch to give the engine lots of air. Water rushed down the portal in waves. It collected on the floor and engaged the sump pumps. I didn't like the sight or sound of the water coming in, but so long as the pumps kept it in check we'd be okay. I cranked the engine all the way up and took my seat on the bicycle. It was going to be a very rough ride.

A short while later the radio connection was lost. While that *was* worrisome, I knew it was probably just the storm. The problem was, they wouldn't be staying in one place. They were drifting with the current and being pushed around by the wind, and I couldn't know which way they were going until they came up on radar. I could only head straight for the coordinates they had given me. If I guessed they had drifted north, when they had actually gone south, I would miss them altogether. I had to go to where they were and hope they hadn't drifted more than ten miles by then.

The pills helped, but not completely. After an hour of a punishing ride I had a headache and seasickness. How I wished we could have dived and sailed by battery. But that just wasn't fast enough. I watched Seaweed struggle to get

comfortable until he got so fed up he hopped onto my swinging bed, and settled down there.

After two hours I thought I was close to their original co-ordinates but there was no sign of them on the radar. That could have meant a number of things but I chose to believe they had simply drifted out of range. I had to pick a direc-tion and search for them, and fast. Securing myself with the harness, I attempted to drop a line overboard to determine the direction of the current. But that was impossible be-cause the storm was tossing us around too much. And the wind seemed to be coming from every direction and pulled on the line this way and that. In general, I knew the current was coming from the south, except that there were places where it spun around differently. And then, the force of the wind was so strong it might even push a small boat against the current.

There was no time to waste; I climbed back inside and turned north. After ten minutes there was no sign of them. After fifteen, still no beep on the radar. At twenty minutes I couldn't stand it; I turned around and headed back. I kept trying the short-wave but there was nothing but static. Twenty minutes of going south I knew we weren't exactly where we were before because of the current. It was now almost three hours since I told them I was coming. I felt a terrible sickness in my stomach, which was not from the seasickness. The thought that I had missed them — that they might have drowned — horrified me. I tried not to think of

it and kept sailing south. And then . . . a faint beep on the radar.

"We found them, Seaweed!" I yelled. "We found them!"

They were ten miles southwest. I pointed in that direction and kept my eyes on the radar. At nine miles I could tell already they were drifting south. Each mile after that I corrected our course to intercept them.

"Hold on!" I yelled, even though no one could hear me but Seaweed.

The sea was nothing but walls of water through the periscope. When I climbed the portal it was the same, except that I could also see the sky, a whirling gray mass of wind and rain. As we approached their location I realized I had to be careful not to run into them. But I couldn't see them. Where *were* they?

Then I thought I saw something. The thing was, I was expecting to see a sailboat. It never occurred to me it might be upside down. Not only had it capsized; it was almost entirely under water and not easy to spot. But there, clinging to its hull, and to each other, were four people. They were wearing sea jackets and life jackets. They had tied themselves together with rope and were half lying across the hull on their stomachs. Every wave was washing over them and they looked exhausted. There were two adults and two children. When they saw me they waved frantically and yelled, though I couldn't hear them.

I took an inflatable buoy and filled it, tied it to a rope,

then tied the other end to the hatch. I came as close as I dared without letting a wave make us collide. It was hard to throw the buoy in the wind. It took six tries before the rope crossed the hull of their boat. They grabbed it and put it over one of their children, then untied her from their ropes. I saw them gesture to her to hold on tightly. Then, they let her go. I pulled as hard as I could. With every pull I wrapped rope around the portal so that it couldn't escape from my hands. Within minutes I had pulled her alongside the sub. She was really young — just six or seven. She was very frightened and crying.

"It's okay!" I yelled. "You're going to be all right!"

I pulled with all my might as she climbed the side of the sub. I climbed out to make room for her. She was shivering uncontrollably and her face was blue.

"You've got to climb inside!" I said.

She didn't bother to look, just obediently put her feet inside and found the ladder. Once I knew she was safe, I pulled the buoy off her.

"Go inside and hold onto something!" I said.

With her frightened face she nodded up at me. I unleashed the buoy rope and began throwing it again. I pulled her brother in. He was about nine or ten years old. Then I pulled their mother. She was a lot heavier but she also pulled herself, so it was much faster.

"Thank you!" she said, with tears running down her face. "God bless you and thank you!"

"You're welcome. It's going to be crowded inside. Hold on to something!"

She nodded as she went down. I unravelled the rope again and threw it for the father. He was very heavy in the water but pulled himself over quickly. As he climbed the sub he looked at me strangely, I think, because of my age. He grabbed my arm and looked into my face.

"Thank you, son."

"There isn't much room inside," I said. "Hold on tight until we dive."

He nodded. He had such a strange expression on his face.

With everyone inside I deflated the buoy and pulled the rope in. I came down the portal, squeezed past the father and son and flipped the hatch switch. The mother and daughter were huddled together around the observation window. Everyone was shivering terribly and their words were broken. I pointed to the space behind the bicycle.

"Please sit there," I said to the father. "We need to distribute our weight evenly."

"Yes, of course."

He sat down.

"If you take your life-jackets off you can sit on them," I said.

"We're fine," said the mother.

"We're going to dive," I said "where it's nice and peaceful. You will see."

"Is it safe?" said the little girl.

"Becky," said her father. "Yes, it's safe. Just do what the captain says."

I filled the tanks and we went down.

"How deep are we going?" said the boy.

"Just a hundred feet," I said.

I engaged the batteries and headed west.

"It's so quiet. We're on battery power, are we?" said the father.

I nodded.

"Yup."

He took off his life-jacket and sea-jacket and nodded to his wife to do the same. They all took them off.

"There's water in here," said the girl.

"There are pumps running, honey," said her father. "They will take all the water away. You will see."

I looked at her.

"That's right."

"Hey!" said the boy suddenly. "There's a seagull on his bed!"

"That's Seaweed," I said. "He's my buddy."

The boy and girl smiled.

"He has a seagull for a pet, Mommy," said the girl.

"I know, dear. It's really nice."

She hugged her daughter tightly.

"Everything's going to be all right now. Everything's going to be all right."

Chapter Eighteen

I made hot chocolate and passed it around with bread and jam. Becky fell asleep on her mother's lap so I coaxed Seaweed off the bed with some bread, and then Jenny, Becky's mom, lay down on the bed with her. Ricky, her son, made himself comfortable in the observation window. He was quite happy to talk to Seaweed, and feed him bits of bread. John, their father, asked me if he could see the engine. I could tell he just wanted to talk privately.

"I suspected nobody would come," he said when we squeezed into the engine compartment. "The storm was too wild. By the time it lessened it would have been too late

for us. It's a miracle you were out there, son."

He shook his head.

"I tried to motor out of it but it kept changing its path and we'd be right in the thick of it again. It chased us for two days."

I didn't know what to say.

"I think I can get you to St. John's in about eight hours. It's hard to say exactly. I've got ten hours of battery power. We could do it faster on the surface but it would be really rough."

"No, this will be just fine."

His lips were trembling and I thought he was going to cry. I hoped he wouldn't.

"I will never be able to repay you for what you did for us."

"I just did what I thought was right. You don't have to repay me anything. There's only one problem."

"What?"

I explained my experience with the coastguard.

"You're the Russian sub! You're the one they're looking for! We heard about you! Oh, isn't that something! Don't you worry, we can straighten *that* out!"

"I don't know if we can straighten it out. First, they'll want to examine my sub, and they'll take a long time doing it; then they'll say it doesn't pass all kinds of official standards and I'll never get it back. All I want is to be free to explore."

"Listen. I know people in the government. I am a lawyer;

I can investigate the legal aspects of this."

"Just the same, I'd feel a lot safer if I could drop you off somewhere where they wouldn't catch me."

"Yes, of course. I understand. Why don't we look at the map and choose a spot?"

We went back and stared at the map. Ricky was trying to play with Seaweed but was falling asleep. I handed John a wool blanket and he put it under Ricky's head.

"You know, it occurs to me that if you handed us over to the coastguard, safely, of course, that it would go a long way to improving your relations with them. Firstly, they would learn firsthand that you are a friendly vessel. Secondly, they would still be able to take responsibility for the rescue, which would make them feel a lot better, since that is part of their job. Do you know what I mean?"

"Yes, I guess so. Do you think they will let me go?"

"I think so, once they catch a glimpse of you. They might request that you report to a certain location at a later time, but, of course, that would be up to you. As it stands now, you are essentially an outlaw; more seriously, a suspected spy. That means the navy is within its right to fire at you, should they deem that necessary. You surely don't want that. Once they realize you are actually a friendly submarine, merely exploring your own coastline, they'll treat the matter quite differently. That's much safer for you, don't you think?"

"I guess so."

To contact the coastguard we had to surface. John piled the life-jackets around Ricky to keep him from rolling around. We went up, but the storm was still raging and I did not open the hatch. The short-wave was still full of static, but it was easier to reach the coastguard. John made the call.

"This is the captain of the sailboat in distress. We have been rescued by a friendly submarine. It is bringing us in. Can you rendezvous? I repeat: this is a *friendly submarine*; can you rendezvous?"

". . . the coastguard," came the reply. "Identify your location."

John looked at me.

"Go ahead."

John gave our coordinates. There was a pause. Then the coastguard replied, "We will rendezvous. Please identify submarine."

"*Domestic* submarine," said John. "From Newfoundland."

I didn't care for the word, "Domestic." I wished he had said, "Exploration submarine."

The coastguard gave us coordinates for the rendezvous — a small bay about twenty miles north of St. John's, only a mile off shore. I decided that once John and his family were off the sub I would quickly dive and pedal to the coast and hide beneath something.

John and I chatted while his family slept. He told me they lived on the Northwest Arm, in the harbour of Halifax, that they moored their sailboat to a private dock at the bottom

of their property, and, that I had to promise to visit them there. He said we could cover the sub with a tarp to hide it from the air. I said I would try to visit. Then he asked me where I was from and how I came to be riding around in a submarine. I told him pretty much everything, without identifying Ziegfried, or giving any hints that could lead to him. John promised to investigate all the legal aspects of my "courageous seafaring," as he called it.

The coastguard beeped loud and clear long before we spotted her. I couldn't believe we were sailing towards the ship that had been chasing me. John was fascinated with the sub now and was enjoying the periscope.

"I see her!" he said. "There she is!"

We got on the short-wave to let her know we were there. They knew already, of course. I surfaced a quarter of a mile away and motored in. The water in the bay was calmer than the open sea but the coastguard was still tossing quite a bit. I was pretty sure it was Joe and Eddie's ship.

A large rescue dinghy was lowered into the water and three sailors climbed into it. The boat had an outboard motor and quickly scooted over to us. One of the sailors appeared to be holding a video camera and was filming everything.

Seaweed was the first one out. He went up the ladder, took a peek at the sky and flew off towards land. I came up, attached myself to the harness and climbed out. I saw Joe in the dinghy and waved, but I don't think he recognized me.

John came up next, climbed out and held onto the hatch. Then, one by one, his family climbed the portal. The dinghy came alongside.

"Please identify the captain of this vessel," said one of the sailors through a megaphone.

I raised my hand in the air.

"Are you the captain?"

I nodded my head.

"Will you surrender your vessel to the coastguard?"

I looked at John, helping Becky out of the portal.

"Don't answer. Just wait until we are in the dinghy and I'll explain it to them. As soon as we're in the dinghy, take off."

The dinghy touched the side of the sub. The sailor threw a life buoy and John put it around Becky, then handed her down and into the dinghy. They did the same for Ricky and Jenny. Finally, John took the sailor's hand and jumped. I untied the harness and went down the portal as fast as I could. I flipped the hatch switch, filled the tanks and went down. At seventy-five feet I turned towards land and started pedalling.

The bay wasn't deep enough to protect the sub from an undertow caused by the storm. It pitched and tossed the way it did above. Coming up just beneath the surface I raised the periscope to see what the coastguard was up to. They sat for about half and hour, then headed south towards St. John's. I pedalled back out and dove to a hundred feet and

settled gently on the bottom. Suddenly I was very tired. It had been quite a night. Changing my damp sleeping bag for dry blankets, I turned the lights low, climbed into bed and made myself cozy. Hopefully my winged friend was cozy somewhere on land.

Chapter Nineteen

The first thing I heard when I woke and turned up the radio was Becky's voice. ". . . and he has a pet seagull and his name is Seaweed."

The news announcer said that the coastguard was still looking for the mystery sub but they no longer considered it a threat. I was relieved to hear that. I made a cup of tea and rose to the surface. In the twilight the wind had calmed but the sea was still churning. I switched on the radar, opened the hatch and motored towards shore, scanning periodically for a glimpse of a now famous seagull. Seaweed had the ability to make friends easily, and would often mingle with a new flock, although he always came as soon as he saw the

sub. Sure enough, one bird separated from a flock on shore and turned my way. Unexpectedly, the rest followed.

Six more birds landed on the sub. Perhaps they thought it was a small island. They didn't care much for its tossing though, and soon flew back to shore. I was glad. The thought of sharing my space with seven seagulls seemed a bit much.

The radar revealed an open sea. But the surface was rough and we had no battery power. And so, I chose a sheltered spot in the bay and ran the engine to recharge the batteries. I shared a breakfast with Seaweed, cleaned my clothes and caught up in my journal.

A few hours later we slipped beneath the waves. Immediately there was a beep on the radar, then another, and yet another. Soon the radar screen was busy with sea traffic. This was the neighborhood of St. John's. There were tankers and freighters coming and going, and smaller craft closer to shore. I felt comfortable enough in the darkness to surface and watch the glow of the city lights as we crossed the harbour. No doubt, the coastguard and navy were in port, but unless they picked us up visually, which was unlikely, they would never know us from any other vessel. How I would have loved to moor somewhere, explore the city and buy a pizza. But such a visit would have to wait.

South of the city, close to shore, the surface was calm enough for sailing. And so I kept the hatch open and the engine running and spent the most pleasurable night cruising down the coast with the radio up loud, my First Mate at my side, and the wind in our faces. All through the night we

watched the lights of shore pass like campfires. We made great time. By the first blue streaks in the sky we had come around the most southern tip of Newfoundland and entered Trepassey Bay. I aimed to tie up close to Portugal Cove, and walk into town. All I wanted was to call Ziegfried, buy some candy, bread and a newspaper. Little did I suspect what was awaiting me.

Finding a secluded spot was easy enough. I tied up to a rock, sealed the hatch and left Seagull on top, or so I thought. Climbing a rocky bluff, I twisted through dense spruce trees and stepped onto the road. Less than a mile away were a few shops, a garage and telephone booth. It was great to hear Ziegfried's voice.

"Alfred! *Finally*! Boy am I proud of you! Who would ever have guessed you would be rescuing people? How ever did you find them in that storm? How did you fit them inside the sub? How are you, anyway? *Where* are you?"

"I'm great. I'm in a tiny town called Portugal Cove."

"Just a minute. Okay, I see it on the map. You're making good time. Everything okay with the sub?"

"Wonderful."

"I see you're still travelling with a seagull."

"Did you hear that on the radio?"

"No, on TV."

"On TV?"

"Yup. They showed you handing over the family to the coastguard. Al, you're famous now. Everybody's talking about it. You're a real hero."

"I don't feel like a hero; I just did what seemed the right thing to do. It wasn't that hard, really."

"Well, I am darned proud of you. And now they know you're not a spy, I don't think they'll bother you anymore. After all, you're a hero. If they caught you, they'd probably have to give you a medal first."

We both laughed.

"How is everything back home?"

"Same as usual. Your grandfather came by. Dropped off some stuff. I think he was just sniffing around. Never said a word."

"I should write them another letter."

"That would be a good idea. You can be sure they've seen you on TV, though, and who knows, that just might just soften them up a bit."

"I hope so. I'd like to visit them when I come back."

While we were talking, I saw two kids walk past and stare at me, but didn't think anything of it. Later, they passed again with another kid. And yet once more. When I got off the phone they approached me. They were about my age.

"Hey! You're the guy with the submarine."

"What? No, that's not me. I just look like him."

"Oh yah? Then why's that seagull following you around?"

"What seagull?"

They pointed to the top of the telephone booth. There, looking like nobody's business, was Seaweed.

"That's just a seagull," I said.

I started to walk towards the store. They followed me. Inside, I quickly chose some bread, pop and candy. When I brought it to the cash the cashier held up the newspaper and pointed to the picture on the front page.

"That's you!" he said excitedly.

"No, it's not. It just looks like me."

"Oh yah? Then where are you from? You're sure as heck not from here. I know everybody around here."

I dug into my pocket for the money. I just wanted to hurry out of there and run back to the sub. Outside were now six kids, including two older ones.

"Where's your submarine?" they said. "We want to see it. Can we have a ride in it?"

I took a deep breath and started to walk down the road, but they stayed with me. Seaweed hopped to the ground ahead of me and squawked. He saw me come out of the store with bread. I pretended I didn't see him.

"Aren't you going to feed your seagull?" said a girl.

"It's not my seagull," I insisted. "But I don't mind giving it a piece of bread."

I opened the loaf and threw Seaweed a slice. He gobbled it and looked for more.

"Where's your submarine?" they kept asking. "We want a ride."

I kept walking. We were only half a mile away but I didn't know how to get away from them. If I started running they would certainly follow, and likely some of them would keep

up with me. I couldn't run as fast while I was carrying the bag, and certainly didn't want to throw it away, so I just kept walking and hoped they would stop following me. The thought of a bunch of kids getting inside the sub and throwing all the switches really scared me. Besides the chance of damaging it, it could be very dangerous for them. Who knows what would happen if they all squeezed inside and started diving? I considered inviting them one at a time, but, truth was, I didn't trust them.

We were almost at the point where I had climbed out of the trees. Seaweed was walking along behind us looking more like a loyal dog than a seagull. I had to think of something fast.

"Do you know where I can go pee?" I said, stopping suddenly.

"You have to go *pee?*" said a girl.

"Go in the woods," said one of the boys.

The idea that I had to pee created a little distance between us, which is what I was hoping.

"I'll hold your *bag,*" said the boy, with a bossy voice. "That way you won't *run* away."

"I'm not going to *run* away. I just have to pee."

I reached into the bag and slipped some of the candy into my pocket, then handed the bag to him. I figured I could get some bread and pop later but I really wanted the candy now. I entered the woods.

"Don't go far! Or we'll come too."

"Don't!" I said, trying to sound as normal as possible.

I went into the woods a short ways, took a few deep breaths, and then . . . took off! I ran as fast as I could, which wasn't easy with all the trees in the way. I heard them yelling and coming after me.

"Catch him! Catch him!"

I tripped twice and bruised my knee. Branches scratched my face and arms. But I made it to the rocky bluff first. I scrambled halfway down the bluff and saw two of the boys closing in. I turned, took a careful look at the water and made a swan dive. It was really cold. Soon I heard two more splashes as the boys followed me. I couldn't believe how determined they were.

Because I was running so hard there was no way I could hold my breath for two minutes, but I knew I could hold it a lot longer than they could. So, instead of coming right up where they could see me, I swam underwater towards the sub. It was probably forty-five seconds or so when I raised my head for air.

"There he is! He's over there!"

The kids on shore climbed back up the bluff while the boys in the water swam in my direction. The sub was just around the corner. I took a few deep breaths and dove again. I felt stronger underwater than on the surface. Besides, they couldn't see me.

I reached the sub at the same time the kids came out of the woods right above it.

"There it is!" they screamed. "The submarine! Hurry! Catch him before he gets away!"

I scampered up the side, jumped down the portal and flipped the hatch switch, but there was no way to keep them from climbing on, which they did. I felt them jump from the rock and land on the bow, and the two boys in the water climb up the side.

Inside, I debated what to do. If I sailed out to sea, some of the kids might stay on, and that would be too dangerous for them. Better to dive first, wait until they let go, and then go out. The only thing that worried me was — what if some of them couldn't swim?

I decided to go down as slowly as possible and watch them through the periscope. At three feet, four kids were still holding on and two were making their way up the rocks. At five feet, two more kids were swimming away and two were still holding on to the periscope and making funny faces in it. At ten feet they were holding their breath. I waited another minute, engaged the batteries and sped a short distance away, then surfaced to periscope level. The six kids were all on shore now and were throwing rocks. Afraid they might hit the periscope, I pulled it down and went out a quarter of a mile, surfaced completely and waited for Seaweed. The kids saw me and danced and waved wildly. I waved back. I realized it wasn't really *me* they were chasing or waving at; it was the excitement of the submarine, and the fact that it was on the news.

Out of the sky, Seaweed appeared and landed on the hatch beside me. I heard the kids cheer from shore. I waved once more, coaxed Seaweed inside, then went beneath the waves. Pulling the soggy candy from my pocket, I wiped the salt water off and put one in my mouth. Seaweed squawked for his share.

"I'm not sure you deserve this, Seaweed," I said, tossing him a candy. "You have to be more careful. Life's going to be more difficult now that we're famous."

Chapter Twenty

The ferry from Argentia, Newfoundland, to North Sydney, Nova Scotia, took fourteen hours. It left in the late afternoon and arrived first thing in the morning. I was planning to follow it. Ziegfried claimed that following closely behind another vessel would take thirty percent less power, or, allow you to go that much faster. What I really wanted was to follow so closely we would appear on radar as one vessel.

I would pedal into port, sneak in underneath the ferry and wait, then follow it out on battery power. Once we were at sea and it turned dark, I would surface behind the ship,

turn on the engine and let the ferry pull me to Nova Scotia in its wake. In theory it was a great idea. There were just a few things I didn't consider.

I waited outside the dock and watched through the periscope as the ferry arrived. While it unloaded, I submerged and slipped in underneath. My first mistake became immediately clear: the enormous engines of the ferry sent waves of sound vibration that nearly drove me crazy. Seaweed wasn't too happy about it either. We endured it for over two hours before the ferry even began to move. Once we were pointed out to sea we rose enough to benefit from the ferry's drag but not enough to be spotted. That's when my second mistake became evident: riding in the turbulence of the ferry's wake was like riding in a storm.

My third mistake came shortly after. Following so closely, yet unable actually to see, I couldn't prevent the possibility of colliding with the ship, which we did, just once. It was just a tap, really. The nose of the sub bumped the stern of the ship like a mouse stumbling into an elephant. I don't know if anyone on the ferry heard it or not, but inside the sub it was *loud*. By the time darkness settled and we rose to the surface and engaged the engine, my nerves were shot. I couldn't stand the vibrations anymore, and the stress of trying to follow so closely, without actually banging into the ship again, was exhausting. The problem was, if I backed off at all, the ferry would suddenly pick us up on its radar and would almost certainly radio the coastguard to say they

were being followed by an unidentified underwater vessel.

After five hours of the most punishing ride imaginable, I simply shut everything off and let the sub drift dead in the water. When the ferry was ten miles away, I turned the engine on again and continued on our way. I knew there was a lesson in all that, but needed time to think about it.

It was not North Sydney I wanted to reach anyway but Louisburg. Once we spotted land, I veered south and followed the coast around Scaterie Island, into the mouth of Louisburg Harbour, where the great fortress lay. Louisburg had been a powerful French military and fishing outpost in the eighteenth century, until the British attacked and destroyed it — twice! Now, much of it had been rebuilt as a museum. Not only did I want to visit the fortress itself, I wanted to explore the waters around it. Thousands of ships had gone in and out of the harbour for years; no doubt some of them had sunk. Who knew what treasures were lying around waiting to be discovered?

The Nova Scotia coast was low-lying and gentle — nothing at all like the rocky bluffs of Newfoundland. The water was also much shallower in places, so I had to keep a close eye on the sonar to avoid striking bottom or running into rocks. As the sun was rising I found a small cove and submerged to fifty feet to sleep. I set the alarm clock to wake me in the early afternoon for time to explore the fortress in the daytime.

Seaweed squawked a few seconds before the alarm went

off. We ate a quick breakfast, rose to the surface and tied up to some rocks. It was starting to turn really cold now, and I wore a warm jacket and hat, partly to disguise myself. As I climbed up on shore, Seaweed took to the air. I had no doubt I would see him soon enough.

Coming through the woods, I crossed a long field and slipped in among the reconstructed buildings. It was dead quiet. Tourist season was pretty much over, but there were clusters of people here and there walking through the buildings and climbing the fortress walls. People were brought in on a bus and had to walk from where they were dropped off to enter the fortress. There they met soldiers and townspeople of the eighteenth century, who were really convincing.

For a couple of hours I just drifted in and out of the buildings, chatted with the costumed housekeepers and warmed myself in front of open-hearth fires. Then I climbed the fortress walls and stared out over the swamp from which the English had come. I had seen the Fortress of Louisburg on TV, and read about it in books, but the real thing was much better.

I went back into the town and peeked inside the door of an eighteenth-century restaurant. The smell of home cooking was too much for my poor belly, and I stepped inside and looked around. A stern-looking lady in a big apron came out and stood in front of me.

"We're closing. Are you with a school group?"

"No."

"Your parents?"

"No."

She looked at me strangely.

"Here by yourself? Are you lost?"

"No. I'm just enjoying the smell."

"Enjoying the smell?"

She looked at me from head to toe.

"Sit down," she said.

It sounded like an order.

"I don't think I have enough money."

I reached into my pocket.

"Sit down!" she barked.

This time it *was* an order.

Her name was Angelina. She told me to wrap a large cotton napkin around my neck; she was going to bring me some pea soup.

"Do you like pea soup?"

"I don't know. I've never had it."

"You never had *pea soup*?"

"Nope."

She clicked her tongue and disappeared. She came back with a large metal bowl filled to the brim. She stood and watched while I took my first sip. A smile spread across my face.

"You like it, eh? It's good, eh?"

I nodded. It was the best thing I ever tasted.

She beamed.

"Keep eating that and don't go away."

Next, Angelina brought me a plate of baked halibut, mashed potatoes, carrots and string beans. I thought I was dreaming.

"You've got a hollow leg," she said.

She brought me apple pie and ice cream next. I gobbled that down almost the way Seaweed ate. Then she brought me a thick piece of gingerbread cake, with whipped cream. I was starting to feel the roundness of my belly. While I ate the last bit of cake, she stared at me closely.

"I think I've seen you somewhere before," she said. "Are you from around here?"

"No."

"Hmmm. You look familiar, but I can't put my thumb on it. Where are you from?"

"Newfoundland."

"Hmmm. No. It's not that."

"I probably just look like somebody else. Other people have told me that."

"Well. We're closing up. The last bus is leaving soon. You'd better skedaddle."

I got up and untied the napkin. My belly was so full I was sleepy.

"Thank you. That was the best meal I ever had."

I really meant it.

"Well, you're welcome."

She paused.

"Just a minute."

She ran into the kitchen and came back with a plastic container and lid, wrapped in a plastic bag.

"Here's some more pea soup. It'll just get thrown out anyway. Take it home and heat it up. Here's some gingerbread too."

I took the bag and put my jacket and hat on.

"Thank you."

"Don't mention it. Now, hurry, or you'll be spending the night inside the fort, and I don't think you want to do that."

Actually, I intended to do exactly that. I left the restaurant, went down the road towards the bus, keeping close to the walls of the buildings. When I saw a narrow alley I ducked into it. I heard someone coming around locking the doors. Before they could see me I ran inside one of the buildings, hid behind some coils of rope and waited. A man came to the door and called, "Anyone inside?"

There was silence. He stepped inside the door. I shut my eyes.

"Anyone? We're closing."

He shut the door and locked it. It was almost dark. Through a second-floor window I saw the twilight. I put my soup and cake carefully on the ground, leaned back as comfortably as possible, and fell asleep.

It must have been a few hours later when I woke to the smell of rope and wood and absolute silence. It was pitch black, and it took me a while to find my bearings. I searched for the soup and gingerbread and found them by my feet. I

pulled them from the bag and shoved them into my jacket pockets. There was no way I was going to leave *those* behind.

A quick search of the building revealed I truly was locked in. But I was able to open a second-floor window and shimmy down with some of the rope. Once on the ground I started to wander around again. A heavy fog had moved in. This made the whole fortress seem, well, kind of spooky. If you happened to believe in ghosts, this wasn't a good place to be. It was lucky I didn't believe in ghosts.

That's what I was thinking when I caught a glimpse of the candle. It was close to one of the buildings and was moving towards me. In the fog I couldn't see anything else. Then it turned into a passageway. I hid behind a corner and stood very still. There must have been workers around still, I thought.

I sneaked around another way, expecting to see the candle in the street. But there was nobody there. There wasn't a single sound, not even a rustling of wind. Then, I heard voices. They sounded distant, as if they were on the other side of a wall. They were speaking French, and were laughing. But there were no lights in any of the windows. Then, at the bottom of the street, I thought I saw one of the old soldiers pass. It was just a silhouette in the fog but it looked like a soldier. I turned around and went down the street. There was no one there! Turning around, I saw the candle again, right where I had just been standing!

I rushed up the street, but kept ready to crouch out of

sight at the first sign of anyone. But there was nothing there, not even the sound of voices that had been there before. I scratched my head. Was I imagining things?

For the next hour I wandered around not seeing or hearing anything. I began to wonder if I had really seen a candle at all. Then, I heard voices coming from the fortress walls, where the dungeons and cellars lay. Peering across the courtyard I saw the candle. This time I went straight after it. Halfway across, it disappeared. A strange fear took hold of me. The closer I went to the walls, the more I felt it, as if there were a force in the walls acting on me. Thirty feet away I stopped. Icy shivers went up my spine. Six ghostly figures came out of a dungeon towards me. They cut the darkness with a single candle. I dropped to the ground and crawled out of the way. But they didn't see me. As they went by, I recognized them, soldiers and ladies, taking a midnight stroll, no doubt in the spirit of Halloween. When they had passed, I caught my breath and laughed. Good thing I didn't believe in ghosts.

In the fog it was difficult to find the sub. I was untying the rope when I heard the most mournful cry imaginable. I wanted to climb inside and get the heck out of there. But what kind of explorer was afraid of a noise in the dark?

Okay, I thought, I'm going to find out where that sound is coming from. I climbed into the sub, engaged battery power and turned towards the center of harbour, in the

direction of the howl. It was loud and pitiful, like someone crying over the dead, except that it didn't sound like a person at all. Neither did it sound like an animal. Suddenly I saw a dory drifting on the water and was hit with a fresh wave of fear. I had always heard of the "old hollies," the cries of a dead fisherman in a drifting dory. When you heard them it meant foul weather was coming. Well, here was a drifting dory that didn't seem to have anyone in it, and the howls coming from it would have woken the dead.

My heart was beating quickly as I came upon it, fully expecting to see something really frightening and ready to jump down and shut the hatch.

"Oooooooooooowwwww!" came the howl.

I was breathing deeply and trying to calm my racing heart as I peered over the side into the belly of the dory. There, right in the middle, with a rope tied around its neck and the other end tied to a stone, was a small dog. He had just opened his mouth to howl again when the sub sneaked up on him. Cowering down with his tail between his legs he peered up at me. I took a deep breath and exhaled.

"Well! You poor thing! What are you doing out here all by yourself?"

Timidly, the little dog began to wag his tail. He was very small — no bigger than Seaweed — and very thin. I had to laugh. I had come face to face with my first ghost.

Chapter Twenty-one

I named him Hollie. He was, without question, the runt of the litter. In fact, if you took a hundred litters and took the runts from each one, then made a litter out of all the runts, Hollie would be the runt of *that* one. He was so ugly he was cute. One of his eyes was a little bigger than the other. One of his ears had been bitten off mostly and the other was twisted sideways like a tree root. His lip didn't quite cover his teeth properly so it always looked like he was either smiling or angry. But he was never angry because he was too timid. Having been afraid of everyone and everything, Hollie never had a chance to develop the capacity to

be angry. I had found him, after all, with a rope around his neck, tied to a stone, which meant that somebody had intended to drown him. Likely they threw him off the wharf and he landed in the dory. But why would they have untied it? Were they so anxious to dispose of him they would throw away an old dory too? Whatever the reason, I felt lucky to have found him. I had always wanted a dog.

But there was one amazing thing about Hollie: he was smart. Whatever he lacked in looks, he made up for in brains. If I pointed to a spot, he would scurry over there and sit. If I said, "Jump!" he would twist his head and stare at me strangely. But when I jumped, he would jump too. Then, the next time I said, "Jump!" he would jump. He loved to learn, and I loved to teach him, although sometimes I wondered who was teaching whom.

I was a little nervous about how Seaweed and Hollie might get along. A dog and a seagull didn't seem likely travelling companions. It wasn't Hollie I worried about; he would have made friends with anyone. But seagulls, as a rule, don't care much for dogs.

I was laying out a blanket in one corner as a bed for Hollie when I heard the unmistakable sound of Seaweed's beak on the hatch. He had a habit of tapping the metal before he hopped down the portal. When he came down and looked around he must have seen Hollie, but he never let on that he did. He simply squawked, which was his way of saying, "Where's breakfast?"

I watched Hollie's reaction. He curled up on the blanket and looked a little worried, as if to say, "You don't expect me to bark at him, do you?"

But Hollie didn't fail to notice that Seaweed received crackers for squawking, so he immediately made a pitiful bark and I threw him a cracker too. Then I learned that sea-gulls and dogs can count. If I tossed either of them more raisins or crackers, I wouldn't get away with it. Even as high as twelve or thirteen, both would know if the other received a single bite more, and would complain bitterly. Otherwise, they tended to ignore each other and keep a respectable dis-tance — except when Seaweed took an interest in Hollie's blanket.

The blanket lay on the starboard side of the observation window and it was the one spot in the whole world that Hollie could call his own. He often left it to run circles around the inside of the sub, as if he were chasing an imag-inary rabbit, but would always return to it, pull it this way and that, then settle like a hen on its nest. Now, Seaweed usually rested on the port side of the window, unless it was stormy, when he would hop onto my bed. But I noticed him inch closer and closer to the blanket until he reached over with his beak and pulled on it, just at the moment Hollie had returned. For one tense moment dog and bird stared at each other, and I wondered if they were going to fight. In-stead, Hollie simply pulled the blanket out of Seaweed's reach. A little while later, the same thing happened again —

Seaweed took hold of the blanket and Hollie pulled it away. The next time, Hollie was lying on the blanket when Seaweed tugged at one corner.

"You're pushing your luck, Seaweed," I said.

Hollie looked up without raising his head and I heard a little growl. It wasn't very loud but it was menacing, with a sense of, "something's-about-to-happen."

Fortunately, Seaweed was smart enough to realize it. After that, Seaweed stayed on his side of the window and Hollie stayed on his.

The waters of Louisburg were indeed a graveyard of sunken ships and junk. But that was no surprise to me because I had seen pictures in the fortress of divers picking the harbour clean of cannon, cannonballs, muskets, pottery shards, dinnerware, and everything else on an eighteenth-century galleon. If there had been any treasure I'm sure they would have found it. All the same, it was exciting to run back and forth across the harbour with the floodlights on and my eyes glued to the observation window. Seaweed watched too and occasionally pecked at the window.

There was something ghostly about the skeleton of a sunken ship. They had often killed people on their way down, and so, in a way, were like murderers. That's what was going through my head when Seaweed started pecking loudly at the observation window.

"What is it, Seaweed? What do you see?"

I strained hard but saw only a few wooden beams criss-crossing over some rocks and broken things — and those were soon out of sight. Without the sun, the water was near-ly as dark as night. The floodlights lit up a narrow circle of light that kept moving as we glided over the seafloor. When we passed the beams, Seaweed stopped pecking. I stopped the sub. He had already proven himself a reliable spotter, so I couldn't ignore his pecking. Putting the sub in reverse, I slowly backed over the same spot. Sure enough, Seaweed started pecking again.

"What is it? I don't see anything."

I decided to turn the sub and come from the side. This gave a different perspective. Sure enough, Seaweed pecked again. I stared and stared but couldn't see anything but wooden beams and debris. I sat and thought about it. The bottom was seventy-five to eighty feet deep in places, and the water was cold. But I *did* have a wet suit.

I figured I'd wait a little while and make one more pass from the other direction. If Seaweed still pecked at the same spot, I'd attempt a free dive.

In the meantime, I made two round piles of cereal on the floor roughly the same size but didn't bother counting the pieces. The crew took a quick glance at each other, then gobbled up the flecks, and, in Hollie's case, licked the floor clean. Neither took the trouble to count.

We made our fourth pass over the beams and Seaweed pecked at the glass as if he were trying to pick something up.

"Okay. I'm going in."

Leaving the floodlights on, I surfaced and suited up. With the flashlight in one hand, I took deep breaths and prepared for a cold shock. Boy! Was it cold! The water seeped into the wetsuit and grabbed my skin with its icy fingers, but warmed quickly as I moved around. The floodlights pierced the water thirty feet or so but didn't reach the bottom. Switching on the flashlight, I continued until I saw one of the wooden beams. The weak glow of the flashlight caught a tiny piece of something shiny, then nothing. I made one sweep of the area, then surfaced. Coming up beneath the sub was like swimming into a halo of light. But on the surface the fog had reduced visibility to zero. I took more breaths and went down again. Once again there was a brief sparkle of reflected light, then nothing. I tried to see it once more before surfacing but couldn't find it. On the next dive I planned to focus on the spot of the reflection but didn't see it. After two more dives I still hadn't seen it. The idea of climbing into a warm bed and listening to the radio was becoming very appealing.

Maybe I'll try one last dive, I thought.

I took breaths and went down with my eyes concentrating hard. This time I saw the glitter — just a tiny fleck of reflected light. I swam beneath one of the beams from where the glitter had come. There was nothing but rocks covered in sea growth. Perhaps the glitter had come from a broken seashell. I was about to surface when the shape of one of the

rocks caught my eye. Unlike the others, it was almost like a box. I gave it a kick. Some debris fell off the side. It wasn't a rock at all; it was a chest!

My heart beat quickly, but I had to surface. When I reached the surface I had to gasp for air and had a slight headache, but I was so excited I felt like yelling. Then I remembered the boxes of sardines and winced. Don't count your chickens before they hatch, I told myself. Besides, I had to figure out how to raise the chest all by myself. It wasn't very big — about the size of a small suitcase — but things underwater had a way of gaining weight.

I climbed into the sub and made some tea to warm up. Probably the best way to raise the chest would be to make a net of rope, wrap it around, then pull it up by winding coils around the hatch. It would be slow, but I could rest in between and not drop it.

I pulled out a hundred feet of rope, sat on the floor and began to fashion the net. My idea was to leave enough space for the net to fit over the box, then quickly tie up the loose ends and secure the chest inside. Of course it had to be done very quickly.

While I worked on one end of the rope, the crew worked on the other. Seaweed seemed to regard the whole thing as some kind of snake and repeatedly attacked it with his beak. Hollie began by pawing the end of it, but quickly fell into a wrestling match with it, rolling around on the floor more like a cat than a dog. Suddenly we heard the distant sound

of seagulls through the open portal. Seaweed responded with an ear-splitting caw. Then he hopped over to the portal and climbed out. Hollie followed him to the bottom of the ladder and watched him go. As Seaweed disappeared, Hollie whimpered and let out a tiny bark. He ran around the inside of the sub looking for another way out, then returned to the portal and barked again. He looked at me with desperation.

"Oh. You need to use the bathroom. I better make you a litter box. But for now you'll just have to go on paper. Here. I'll put some newspaper down in the stern. Go here, Hollie. Go here."

But he just twisted his head in confusion and went back to the ladder and whined.

"I'm sorry, Hollie. If you want out, you're going to have to learn to climb a ladder."

I didn't think he would ever try; he was so small. Seaweed had the advantage of a beak, which allowed him to hang on while he shifted his feet.

Once the net was ready and my belly was warmed with tea, I climbed out the portal and tossed the rope into the water with a weight to pull it down.

"Keep an eye on the sub, Hollie," I said, then went over the side.

The water felt colder because I was growing tired. But I found the chest and managed to wrap the net partly around it before surfacing. At the top I took breaths and called to

Hollie, just to let him know I wasn't far away, then went back down. On the second dive I managed to close the net around the chest. It was hard work. I had to stick the flashlight under one arm and concentrate. At seventy-five feet it felt as if you were moving through mud. But coming up I was very excited. Somehow, I just knew this chest was filled with something better than sardines.

I climbed onto the sub and caught my breath.

"Hollie! I'm back!"

I looked down the portal and waited for the little face to show.

"Hollie! Where are you? I'm back!"

He never showed. That was strange.

"Hollie! Are you sleeping?"

Still there was no answer. I went down and searched everywhere. But he was gone.

Chapter Twenty-two

Hollie had jumped ship. I didn't know what to do. The sub was sitting mid-harbour, surrounded by dense fog and secured by a rope to a chest on the bottom. If I moved the sub, the chest would drag along the bottom, no doubt catching the rope around the beams and pulling them along. Maybe the rope would snap. Maybe the chest would smash open and spill its contents all over the murky bottom.

On the other hand, Hollie was likely swimming around the fog in circles. He must have been out there for five or six minutes already. I had to find him quickly. If I tried to use the sub I wouldn't be able to spot him anyway because I

couldn't steer from the hatch — I could only run in one direction, and that was too risky.

Turning on the hatch floodlights, I took off my diving belt and slipped into the water. Without the belt I floated easily and could swim faster. Calling Hollie's name, I began to swim in widening circles around the sub, using the flood-lights as a kind of lighthouse.

After ten minutes, there was no sign of him and I was worried. Unlike a seagull, a dog wouldn't know which way was shore in a fog. Besides, Hollie was really only a puppy; there was no way he could swim that far.

After twelve minutes I was feeling very discouraged. When I had told him he would have to learn to climb the ladder I was only kidding. It never occurred to me he might really try.

After thirteen minutes I could barely see the light of the sub. It seemed so hopeless. I felt absolutely terrible. I had rescued a dog only to put him in a worse situation. I yelled one more time — my voice cracking with emotion. And then, I saw a tiny little head coming through the water towards me.

"Hollie! Oh! Come here!"

He reached me exhausted. I rolled onto my back and lifted him onto my belly. He collapsed onto his side but reached up and licked my chin.

"You crazy little dog! You are too smart for your own good!"

Finding Hollie — for the second time — meant more to me than finding any treasure chest. I carried him inside, dried him off and settled him on his blanket. Then, I explained how he mustn't ever climb out on his own again, but I didn't think he was listening. He just lay flat on his blanket and stared up at me as if to say, "I'm sure glad that's over."

With Hollie safe inside, I went back to the business of raising the chest. Standing behind the hatch, I leaned back and tugged on the rope. The first few pulls were surprisingly easy, but that was because I was only pulling the slack out of it. On the fourth pull I felt the real weight, not only of the chest, but the rope as well. By leaning completely backwards, so that I was hanging out over the water, and by pushing with my legs against the portal, I could just barely pull the rope. At seventy-five feet — raising it about two and a half feet each pull — I knew I had to make at least thirty pulls. That didn't seem so bad, especially since I could rest in between. It was easier somehow to count the pulls out loud, knowing that with each one the number was becoming smaller.

At twenty pulls my arms were sore. At thirty they were aching but there was no sign of the chest. Then it occurred to me — my pulls were getting shorter. I decided to go inside and see how Hollie was doing. He was asleep — wrapped up in his blanket. As I opened a can of peaches and started eating, there were two beeps on the radar.

"Oh no! Not *now*!"

The vessels were coming from shore. They must have been a couple of fishing or motor boats. They weren't coming directly towards us but were sweeping in two arcs, as if looking for something. I hurried outside and resumed pulling. Thirty-five, thirty-six, thirty-seven pulls — suddenly the rope stopped. I looked over the side. There, lying nearly the length of the sub, was one of the wooden beams! I had to laugh. Running back inside, the radar revealed that the boats were closing in. I went out and unhooked the beam from the rope and watched it sink. The chest was still inside the net. Suddenly I saw two lights appear in the fog.

"Hey!" yelled a man. "A submarine! Hey! It's that outlaw submarine!"

I heard other men yelling. They were very excited.

"Hey! What are you doing?"

I didn't answer. The thought of losing the chest to strangers did not appeal to me at all. But there was no time to try to bring it inside. Instead, I jumped down the portal and reached for the controls.

"Hey!" came the voices. "Wait! What's going on here?"

I started the engine, raised the throttle to full speed and aimed for the open sea. Then I ran back up the portal and saw one man perched on the bow of his boat, getting ready to jump to the sub.

"Wait!" he cried. "Wait! What are you doing here? Wait a minute!"

Just as he was just about to jump, I shut off the sub's

floodlights, putting the sub in darkness. The small lights from the motor boats were aimed at us but were not enough for the man to jump safely. I looked down to see the rope and chest twist and turn as the sub plowed through the water. I just hoped it would stay intact long enough for us to get away.

They chased us for five miles. Evidently they weren't outfitted with radar. I could tell because they just went straight out and didn't follow us when we made a southward turn. All the same, I had to put more distance between us because the fog was lifting.

Four miles away, I brought the sub to a halt and climbed out. The chest was still dangling in the net. If I lost it now I would never find it again — the water was too deep. But I was too afraid to drag it any further; sooner or later it would either slip through the rope, or start breaking apart in the pounding waves.

Raising the chest alone was a lot easier than pulling the beam too. However, lifting it out of the water was much harder. Once I started, I couldn't stop, not even to run below and check the radar. I just hoped they wouldn't spot the sub. Unfortunately, they did. The chest was only halfway up the side when I saw them coming again — two motorboats. I secured the rope to the hatch, climbed inside and took off again. This time at least the chest was not getting hit by waves. But the pursuers got a very clear look at what I was doing.

With the sub pointed out to sea, I attached myself to the

harness and climbed out and resumed pulling the chest. I knew they could see me still but I had no choice. I couldn't dive until the chest was safely inside, or I would lose it.

It was such hard work but I raised the chest to the top of the hatch. Then, unwinding the rope slowly, I lowered the chest inside the portal. Once it was on the floor, I untied the rope, climbed inside, shut the hatch, cut the engine and dove to a hundred feet. The radar showed the motorboats spinning in circles above. Eventually they stopped. I engaged the batteries, turned around 180 degrees and collapsed on the floor. I had to go back for Seaweed. Little did my pursuers suspect, I was following them back to their own harbour.

Water continued to leak out of the chest for quite a while — like an ice cube melting. Beneath rust and barnacles and crustaceans I saw the unmistakable blue fleur-de-lis, the French symbol that was all over Louisburg. Around the edges were strips of metal, which had reflected the light. On the front was a lock, rusted beyond use. But the chest didn't look difficult to open, especially as Ziegfried had outfitted the sub with an excellent store of tools.

First, I cut the lock with a hacksaw, although it mostly came apart in my hands. Then, I loosened the lid with a chisel around the inside of the edge. The hinges at the back — rusted shut — simply shattered when I raised the lid. Inside I saw rows of forks and knives and spoons — silver and gold. They were tarnished but elegant. I didn't know if it

was real gold and silver, but it sure looked like it. Rows of cutlery — that was the treasure. I sat back and stared. Well, if it were real gold and silver, then it really was valuable. Besides, it must have been worth something just for being so old. It wasn't the most exciting treasure to find — forks and knives and spoons — but it was still treasure.

Then I noticed something else.

There was something about the chest that didn't look right, but I couldn't tell what it was. I stared for a long time, trying to figure it out. We were approaching Louisburg harbour again so I left the chest and sat at the control panel. On the radar I watched the motorboats return to their dock. Rising to periscope level I saw the fog finally clearing in the harbour. It was time to get some sleep. Diving to seventy feet, I turned the lights low and crawled into bed. Hollie was sleeping soundly. From my bed I could see the chest. I stared at it, trying to figure out what was so peculiar about it, but sleep quickly overcame me.

Chapter Twenty-three

"The submarine outlaw has been spotted in Louisburg harbour," said the news announcer as I woke.

Wow! I thought, News travels fast!

"No one knows why he was in the harbour," said the announcer, "but he may have been treasure-hunting, according to local boaters."

"We chased him," came the excited voice of a man. "We chased him clear out of the harbour and twenty miles out to sea. But he got away. He slipped beneath the water just like an eel and that was the last we saw of him. He's probably on his way to Portugal by now."

I had to smile at the twenty miles part. How surprised they would be to know we were still in their harbour. I turned my head to look at the chest and suddenly guessed its secret — the bottom on the inside was higher than the outside. It held a secret compartment!

I climbed out of bed and heated water for tea. Hollie jumped up with his tail wagging, as if to say, "What are we going to do today?"

"We're going to pick up the rest of the crew and head for sea, that's what we're going to do. But first I'm going to examine the chest."

There didn't seem to be any way to open the hidden space, and nothing rattled when I shook it. I lightly tapped the edges with a hammer and chisel, hoping the bottom plate would pop out, but it wouldn't. Hollie came over and stared into the chest.

"Can *you* open it?" I asked.

He looked at me in his nervous way, reached out a paw and touched the top of the chest. We both looked inside. Nope, nothing. He came around to the other side and stood up on two legs and leaned against it.

"I could cut it open, but that would make a mess, and I'd rather leave it as it is."

Hollie picked up the chisel in his mouth, stood up on the chest and dropped it inside.

"I tried that already."

But when the chisel landed, it loosened the floor beneath

it just slightly. I picked it up and dropped it again. The floor loosened a little more. Suddenly, I could see that what looked like the floor of the chest was really just a thin wooden board, very tightly fitted into the sides. It couldn't be pulled out, it had to be cut, but it was only a board — I didn't mind cutting that.

With one edge of the chisel I began to cut a trench right down the middle. I worked delicately, so as not to damage whatever was beneath. Eventually I was able to pull the board out in two pieces. Underneath was yet another chest, very flat and tightly fitted into the bigger one. It had a lock built into it but was also rusted beyond use. The small chest was so tight I had a hard time freeing it. When I finally pulled it out I was too anxious to figure out how to open it properly and simply cut around the lid with a hacksaw. Lifting it, I saw gold coins neatly fitted into a bed of wood and held in place with straps. There were twenty of them.

"Hollie, I think maybe we're rich."

Hollie gave me his paw. He was very pleased.

The coins were larger than our coins, and a *lot* heavier. I didn't know anything about old coins but I bet they were worth a lot. I couldn't wait to tell Ziegfried. I planned to give him half. Now there would be lots of money for food and fuel and everything else.

In the early twilight I raised the periscope in the middle of harbour. There was no way to know if Seaweed had seen it or not. It was too risky to surface before dark. So I waited.

Coming up slowly, I kept an eye on the radar. Then, cautiously, I lifted the hatch. Sure enough, my faithful first mate was there.

"Tuna fish?" I said.

It was a good night for sailing. The waves were moderate, the wind mild and the sky clear. But the air was cold. I had to wear my jacket and hood whenever I stood in the portal. There wasn't much traffic — a couple of beeps on the radar seven or eight miles out. Passing freighters, no doubt. I decided to look for a spot close to Canso, a town big enough to use a telephone without getting noticed, or so I hoped.

At first it was difficult to find a place secluded enough for the sub. Then, I spotted an old abandoned boathouse. The water was merely fifteen feet deep, but enough for the sub. Gliding in, I felt like an airplane landing on an aircraft carrier. Raising the hatch and seeing a roof overhead was really strange.

The boathouse was at the bottom of a hill. The field had been fallow for many years. To the right was a dirt road that looked as though it hadn't been used in a long time. With Hollie under one arm, I climbed out, sealed the hatch and squeezed through a crack in the boathouse wall. Seaweed followed and took to the air. Hollie's legs were spinning before I put him down, and he hit the ground running. He was so excited he ran all the way up the road and back. He ran into the field and around and around in circles. He ran like

a windup toy that never stops. But when I reached the top of
the hill and called him, he came immediately. Together we
walked along the road into town. I pulled the collar of my
jacket up and my hat down and hoped that if anyone saw
us they would be distracted by Hollie and not notice me.

But we didn't see anybody, only a car or two. We came
into a corner of the town, found a phone booth and called
Ziegfried. But there was no answer. That was strange. Ziegfried was always home, especially in the early morning. I
waited for awhile and tried again. Hollie squeezed into the
booth with me. I looked up to see if Seaweed was sitting on
top. He wasn't. After five more tries I still couldn't reach
Ziegfried. Something must have come up.

Across the street was a corner store, and there was no one
around. The thought of returning to the sub with a bag of
candy was too tempting to resist. Besides, if anyone *did* chase
me I certainly wouldn't lead them to the sub again. Coming
up the steps to the store, I peeked inside. There was just one
man sitting at the counter reading the paper. I opened the
door and followed Hollie in.

"Good morning!" I said.

"'Morning!" said the man, without looking up.

He was too busy with the paper to care about us. I went
to the cooler and picked out a large bottle of pop. Then I
went to the candy shelf and chose a whole bunch of different things. It occurred to me that this would be the first year
I would not receive anything for Halloween, except what I

bought myself. On the way to the counter I grabbed two loaves of bread and a bag of dog biscuits. Hollie's tail was wagging happily. I knew Seaweed wouldn't turn his beak down at a dog biscuit either.

At the cash, the man counted our things without taking his eyes out of the paper. I wondered what was so interesting. Straining to read upside down, I made out the words, "... submarine outlaw ... Louisburg ..."

"Is it going to rain today?" I said quickly.

"Who knows?" he said. "That'll be ten fifty."

I handed over eleven dollars. He took the money. Suddenly he looked up and stared at me.

Oh, oh! I thought. Here it comes.

"Dogs aren't allowed in the store."

"Oh. Sorry. I'll leave him outside next time."

He handed me my change and dropped his eyes to the paper.

"Bye," I said.

He never answered. Hollie and I left the store.

"Whew! That was easy."

On the way back to the sub we had a great time eating candy and dog biscuits. Halfway, Seaweed dropped out of the sky. He saw Hollie eating something and immediately demanded his share. So, the three of us followed the road to the hill and down the dirt road to the boathouse. It was a fresh autumn morning and I thought how wonderful life could be.

The eastern shore of Nova Scotia grew more beautiful the further south we went. This was so because of the changing leaves and endless small islands. Passing islands at night was like drifting by sleeping sea monsters, with just a few lights for eyes. In the morning, with the rising sun, the islands burst into flaming red, orange and yellow colours that made us grin with excitement. Well, Hollie was always grinning. I stood in the portal while he balanced on my shoulder — his front legs on the hatch. Seaweed would hop onto the bow and the three of us face into the wind, watching the candy-coloured islands go by. There were few that we could land on because there were so few approachable coves, but occasionally we did find an uninhabited island on which to moor the sub and disembark. On some of those we brought out the tent, made a beach fire and slept on land, which was the strangest feeling after having grown so used to the sea. Hollie, in particular, seemed to enjoy the endless space and the freedom to roam.

But two things were drawing me to Halifax with growing interest: I had promised to visit the family I had met in the storm; and I wanted to investigate the treasure. It would be nice to spend time with people who wouldn't chase me. And, as much as I loved being at sea, the thought of sitting around a table with friends and pizza, and maybe going to see a movie, seemed like a lot of fun. I could also visit a library and read about old coins, maybe even get an expert's opinion on what they were worth.

John had drawn a detailed map to their property. He said he would leave a rolled tarp on the dock, ready for covering the sub when I came in. Their home was on the Northwest Arm, which he said was too shallow for coming in submerged. We would have to sneak in on the surface at night. Halifax, itself, had one of the deepest harbours in North America, and was a naval port. That meant there were military people sitting at screens watching every movement above and below the surface of the water. There was no way we could even attempt to come near Halifax below the surface. Above, they might think we were any other small boat; below, they would *know* we weren't.

Shortly after dark we sailed out of Musquodoboit Harbour, where we had spent the day. Two miles offshore, we sneaked along the surface at the speed of a sailboat coming in by motor. We passed Lawrencetown, Cole Harbour, and turned the corner of Eastern Passage, where we saw the lights of freighters and tankers and tugboats coming in and out of Halifax. It was exciting to enter such a busy harbour. Standing in the portal with Hollie, as we passed McNab's Island, I had the Northwest Arm almost in sight. Everything was going smoothly, until a beam of light swung across our bow. It came from one of the tugboats returning to port. The light bounced off the hull, swept in an arc and returned. They spotted us! They must have seen us on radar and wondered why we weren't carrying lights. I should have known better. Jumping down the portal, I flipped some

switches, sealed the hatch, dove to a hundred feet and shut everything off. Now we were where we didn't want to be — underwater in a harbour with sophisticated sonar. Realizing my mistake, I rose again to just a couple of feet below the surface — to appear on their sonar as a surface vessel, not a submerged one — and raised the periscope. The tugboat had veered in our direction and was scanning the water. Climbing onto the bicycle I pedalled as fast as I could and steered around the approaching tugboat. Whether or not they detected us I never knew. I just kept pedalling towards the Northwest Arm with all my might.

The seafloor rose considerably as we approached the Arm — a narrow and shallow strip of water bordered by trees and houses. I turned on the sonar and quickly learned that John was right: we had to surface to cover the last half-mile to their home. It was the middle of the night when we found the little dock. Climbing out, I saw two small moored sail-boats, with a space between them just big enough for the sub. Squeezing into the middle, I found the tarp and pulled it over the portal and hull. Now it looked like three sailboats — one under tarp. I looked around to see if we had been followed. For the moment, we appeared to be home-free.

Chapter Twenty-four

There were ghosts in John's backyard and a witch on the side of the house. The witch had crashed in a high wind. I laughed when I saw it. I didn't want to wake anyone but thought we could sit on the step and watch the night turn into day. This was something I had never anticipated — becoming a nocturnal being, like a bat or an owl. There was something very nice about it, watching the sun go up and down and the seasons change, while everybody was sleeping.

There was a wrap-around veranda on the house, with a hanging swing. I sat down on the swing and Hollie jumped

up beside me. He stared up at me in his nervous little way and I stroked his good ear. Together we watched the wind tear the straggling leaves from the trees and race them away into the darkness. We watched for a long time, and listened, and then we fell asleep.

We must have looked a lonely picture, because when I woke, I saw the whole family staring at us with something like pity.

"Alfred!" said Jenny, "Why didn't you wake us? You shouldn't be sleeping out here! Come in this instant and get warmed up and have some breakfast!"

"Oh, we weren't sleeping, really, just watching the leaves. We arrived in the middle of the night and didn't want to wake anybody."

"You found the dock all right then, did you?" said John.

"Yes, it was no problem. But I think we were spotted in the harbour last night."

"We know!" they all said.

"You know?"

"We heard it on the news this morning."

"On the news *already*? Man, news travels fast!"

"You're famous, Alfred," said Jenny. "Everybody wants to catch a glimpse of the submarine outlaw."

"Yes, especially us!" said Ricky.

"Yah, especially us!" said Becky. "Where did you get the cute little doggie?"

She started patting Hollie, who looked up at me to see if it was okay.

"I found him . . . in a boat."

"Did you *rescue* him?" said Ricky.

"Well, sort of. Somebody tied him to a stone."

"Then you *rescued* him," said Jenny.

Jenny looked as though she was going to cry.

"Come inside, Alfred. Please," said John.

Hollie and I jumped off the swing and followed them in.

"Alfred," said Becky, taking my hand, "you rescue *everybody*."

Jenny sat me at the table while she cooked the most delicious breakfast ever made. She made scrambled eggs and french toast and bacon and fresh orange juice and tea. Everyone sat around the table and talked excitedly, but I couldn't help noticing that Jenny sometimes started to cry, without warning, yet never stopped doing what she was doing. Nobody else seemed surprised by it.

"Don't pay any attention to my tears," she said later. "It's just post-traumatic-stress-syndrome. It's one way of saying that I'm really happy we are all still alive. Seeing you, Alfred, has a strong effect on all of us. You will never know how grateful we are that you found us that terrible night, when we thought we were lost."

I didn't know if it was also part of the traumatic-stress-syndrome or not, but Jenny kept hugging me a lot. I didn't really mind, I guess, although I never knew what to do. I wasn't used to getting hugs. Sometimes when she hugged me I could feel she was sobbing inside, although she tried not to show it.

"Let's show him the presents!" said Becky, excitedly.

"Let him eat first," said John. "Then we'll show him."

"We bought you presents," said Ricky. "Each of us was allowed to choose one really nice thing."

"You didn't have to buy me presents."

"I'm afraid you'll just have to accept that it's something we wanted to do," said John.

"Yes," said Jenny, "It's just that . . ."

She wasn't able to finish her sentence.

"It's just that we wanted to say thank you," said Ricky.

"I can't wait till you see what I picked out for you, Alfred," said Becky.

"Let him eat first," said John.

"What's your doggie's name?" said Becky.

"Hollie. I found him. I thought he was a ghost."

"You thought he was a ghost?" said Becky, scratching his head. "That's funny."

"He's really smart," I said.

"Hey! Where's your seagull?" said Ricky.

I looked out the window.

"Oh, he's probably sitting on the tarp. I don't think he likes houses."

After breakfast the kids led me upstairs. John and Jenny stayed behind to chat about something. Then they came up behind us.

"Presents time!" said Ricky.

I followed them into a bedroom, where five wrapped

boxes stood on the floor. They had brightly coloured ribbons and bows.

"This is *your* room now, Alfred," said Becky.

"What Becky says is true, Alfred," said Jenny. "We want you to have this room. You can come and go, as you like. We will keep it for you."

"Really? But . . ."

I didn't know what to say.

"Open your presents!" said the kids.

"Open mine first," said Becky.

I picked it up.

"This is really heavy."

"Open it!" she said. "You're going to like it. It's something you can use."

Carefully, I pulled off the bow, unwound the ribbon and tore the tape free of the paper. Inside was a brown cardboard box. Inside that, were a number of smaller boxes. I opened one.

"It's a movie camera!" said Becky. "Now you can take movies of all the places you go."

"Wow! It's wonderful! Thank you! What a great idea!"

"It has batteries too," said Becky. "And extra tapes and other stuff."

I opened the box and took the camera out. It looked very fancy and very expensive.

"Now mine!" said Ricky.

I handed the video camera to Becky and started opening

Ricky's gift. Inside was another video recorder.

"Another one?"

"An *underwater* video camera," said Ricky. "For making movies underwater."

"Wow! That's amazing! You guys chose the very best presents ever. I am going to make great movies and then show them to you."

"Can we come out on your submarine again sometime?" said Ricky.

"You bet! If your mom and dad say so."

I looked at Jenny. There were tears in the corners of her eyes. She smiled.

"Open this one next," she said.

Inside Jenny's present I found a heavy oiled wool sweater, a hat, mitts, pants, boots and a sea parka.

"This is so much stuff! I can't accept all this!"

"Yes, you can," said Jenny.

She lifted the parka out of the box and fitted it around my shoulders.

"I want to know that you are keeping warm when you are out there," she said.

"I think it would be impossible to get cold with this," I said.

"Another present, Alfred," said John.

The next box was the biggest and heaviest one. Opening it, I discovered a tall, silver metallic box. There were pipes and wires coming out of the back. I stared at it for awhile, trying to figure it out.

"It's a fridge and freezer," said John, "for your sub!"

"Really?"

"Really. It hooks up to your batteries. It doesn't take much space. Maybe you can squeeze it into your engine room."

"Now we can give you frozen pies and cakes," said Jenny.

"And you can have ice cream!" said Becky.

"There's one more present," added John.

"It's from *all* of us," said the kids.

I opened the last box and pulled out a smaller silver container.

"It's an on-board microwave," said John. "Now you can heat up those frozen pies."

I looked at all the presents. They were so thoughtful. I really felt I didn't deserve them, but everyone seemed so happy about it.

"Thank you," I said. "I really don't know what to say."

"Don't say anything else," said Jenny. "You'll just make me cry."

Everyone laughed.

I wanted to tell them about the treasure, but somehow it didn't seem like the right time. They were so excited about seeing me and giving me the presents that I decided to wait. But I was too anxious to wait to read up on the coins. So I mentioned that I'd like to go into the city and check something out.

"Oh, we'll give you a ride," said Jenny.

"That's okay, I'd like to walk. It's nice to walk when you've been in a submarine such a long time."

"Oh. I suppose so. Okay. Well, we have a map you can use, and I'll give you our telephone number so you can call if you need anything, okay?"

"Okay."

She looked a little worried.

"Hey," I said. "Would you like to meet up later and maybe get a pizza and go to a movie?"

"Oh, that's a great idea," said Jenny. "John, do you think we could go to a movie?"

"I don't see why not."

"Yay!" said the kids.

We looked through the movies in the paper and chose one. Then John showed me where to find the theatre on the map. We agreed to meet at five o'clock, for pizza.

Hollie kept close to my feet as we walked into the city. I wasn't afraid he would run away; he never went further than my shadow. Whenever we crossed a busy street I picked him up and carried him. In the middle of town we found a park with ducks and geese. Hollie kept a watchful eye on the geese, who were so much bigger than he was. I saw seagulls in the sky and on the ground but never Seaweed. I hoped he would find us when we were leaving.

We found the public library, climbed the steps and were greeted by a sign that read:

NO PETS ALLOWED (except seeing-eye dogs)

"Shoot! Hollie, we're not allowed in."

Hollie looked up, confused.

"I don't think you look like a seeing-eye dog. Hmmm. Maybe if you're really quiet I can sneak you in."

Hollie was *very* quiet, especially around other people or animals. I picked him up and tucked him inside my jacket. He looked up at me as if to say, "Don't worry, I'll be as quiet as a mouse."

I pushed open the door and we went in. First we walked all around, looking at the thousands and thousands of books, but I had no idea how to find books on coins. Then I saw an information desk with a strict-looking lady. With one hand in my jacket pocket, keeping a grip on Hollie, I went up to the desk and asked if she could point me in the direction of books on old coins. The lady looked up at me through old-fashioned glasses and took a while to answer.

"Do I know you?" she said.

"I don't think so."

"Hmmm. You look familiar. Old coins, eh? Sure. Follow me."

She got up and went across the room and down a stairway. We followed her and I realized the library was even twice as big as it looked. She knew exactly where to go and led us to one far corner. Hollie was starting to squirm a little in my jacket.

"This whole row has books on old coins," she said.

"Thank you."

She smiled. As she was leaving she said, "Cute doggie. Keep him quiet, okay?"

I nodded.

"Wow!" I whispered to Hollie, "she was nice."

I took off my jacket and put it on the floor. Hollie climbed onto it, pawed it back and forth, curled up and went to sleep. It had been a long walk for him.

For an hour or so I flipped through books on coins. Every now and then I raised my head. How strange it was to be in a library, surrounded by walls of books, instead of walls of water. In my pocket I carried one of the coins from the chest. I pulled it out to compare, but none of the pictures I saw matched it. It was difficult because my coin was shiny and gold; all the pictures in the books were black and white. Then I realized I had been looking through ancient Greek and Roman coins. One of the books was called, "Old French Coins." Opening that, I came face to face with the coin in my hand. In the book it was called "Le Roi Soleil," which meant "The Sun King." On one side was a picture of an ugly man in a wig; on the other were the words: "L'état c'est moi," which meant, "I am the State." The book said these coins were very rare and were worth upwards from $1,000 each, depending on their condition. I looked at my coin. It was perfect.

Now I knew roughly what the coins were worth. But how did one go about selling them? That was my next stop.

Chapter Twenty-five

E ver since I climbed into the submarine and left Dark
Cove, I had had to make more important decisions on
my own than ever before in my life. What was beginning to
become clear to me was that I seemed equally able to make
bad decisions as well as good. I just didn't know ahead of
time which were the good ones and which the bad. Afterwards, it was always easy to know. Playing with matches on
an oily barge and following a ferry closely were bad; rescuing John's family and facing the "old hollies" were good. I
was about to discover that going into a coin shop with a
rare gold coin in my pocket was bad.

Maybe it was the excitement that clouded my good sense. Or maybe it was that I didn't quite believe what the book had said and wanted the opinion of a real person. Whatever the reason, I went searching for a coin shop with a trusting blindness.

The coin shops didn't just deal with coins. On their signs — and there were several such shops in the same area — they said they bought and sold rare coins, stamps, gold, silver, fridges, stoves, TV's, computers, and just about everything else. They also said that short-term loans were available. Of course I didn't care about any of that. I simply wanted information on a very special coin.

Entering the first shop, with Hollie at my heels, I was surprised to see how messy it was. When the shopkeeper appeared, he didn't look any better. He was picking his teeth with a chicken bone and his belly was bursting out of his shirt. I glanced around the shop and thought that Ziegfried's junkyard was neater.

"Yah?" said the shopkeeper, "what do you want?"

"Oh. Ah . . . nothing. I was just looking around."

"Oh yah? Well go look around somewhere *else*."

I left the shop and went across the street where another shop looked in better shape. Inside, everything was dusty but more or less organized. At the counter a man in glasses was reading a book. Hollie and I approached him. He looked up from his book and scanned us as if we were two bugs on the floor.

"Yes?" he said, in a quiet, dry voice.

"Do you deal in old coins?"

"Yes."

"Um . . . do you buy and sell rare antique coins?"

"Of course. What kinds of coins are you taking about?"

"Um . . . French coins."

"Gold coins?"

"Yes."

His eyes narrowed and he smiled a little.

"We buy and sell them all the time. You'd be surprised how many people want to buy old gold coins. We give the very best price for *French* gold coins."

He reached for a dog-eared catalogue and flipped through the pages.

"What kind of French coins are you talking about, this one?"

He put his finger on the page. I leaned over and glanced at it.

"No, not that one."

He eyed me closely again then looked down at the catalogue.

"Oh. This one then?"

"No, not that one."

"This one, perhaps?"

I looked carefully.

"No, it's none of the coins on that page."

He raised his eyebrows.

"Have you got the coin with you?"

I didn't answer. I looked down and saw Hollie staring up at me nervously. He didn't like the atmosphere of the shop.

"It's not one of those," I repeated.

He took a deep sigh and turned the page.

"Is it one of these coins?" he said, as if he were bored.

The way he pretended to be bored immediately reminded me of something, but I was too excited to pay attention to it. Suddenly I saw my coin at the bottom of the page. It was the very last one.

"There!" I said. "That one!"

He grinned, and his eyes twinkled for just a split second. Then he regained his bored expression.

"Those coins are exceptionally rare. I don't think your coin is that one. Can I see it?"

"Um, no, I don't have it with me."

"Oh. Too bad. Look closely. Are you sure it's the same coin?"

He turned the book around. I read the inscription.

"It's French," he said. "Do you know what it means?"

"I am the State," I said.

His eyes opened round and wide.

"Well, it's too bad you don't have the coin with you. If I could see it I could tell you what it's worth. Perhaps you could go and get it and bring it back?"

"I'll think about it," I said. "Could you give me even a *rough* idea what it might be worth?"

"Oh," he said, with a frown, "it's worth at least a thousand dollars or so, if it's really '*Le Roi Soleil.*' Just a minute."

He disappeared into another room and I thought I heard him using the telephone. Maybe he was calling somebody else to ask. When he returned, he had a friendlier expression on his face.

"Well, I'm sorry I couldn't help you, but if you come back later I'm sure we can do business."

The door opened and two men came into the shop. I don't know how but I instantly knew something was wrong. The two men didn't look around or approach the counter; they just stood there. The shopkeeper didn't pay them any attention.

"Maybe you see something here you like?" he said.

I didn't. It was time to go. Hollie seemed to think so too.

"Maybe I'll come back later," I said.

I had no intention of ever returning. I pulled open the door and Hollie and I went out. We only took a few steps when the door opened again and the two men came out. They saw us and looked the other way. I picked Hollie up and crossed the street. They crossed the street too. My heart started to pound. They were following us!

I thought of going into another shop, but nothing really looked safe. For some reason I headed downhill towards the harbour, even though the sub wasn't anywhere close. I always felt safer close to water. They followed us down the hill. I put Hollie down. When we went around a corner I

started to run a little, just to put more distance between us. When the men turned the corner, they picked up their pace too. I looked around, hoping to see a police car, but the further we went in that direction the more deserted it was. To the left I saw the tugboat dock; to the right, the container terminal, where the big ships docked. In between were a few abandoned buildings, parking lots and old piers. The quickest way to reach the water was across a parking lot and alongside an empty building. Crossing another street, I picked up Hollie and started to run as fast as I could. Looking back, I saw the men running too. But they weren't coming fast — probably because they knew there was nowhere for us to go.

When we reached the edge of the pier I put Hollie down.

"Run! Hollie! Quick! Run!"

I pointed the way for him to go but he just looked up at me, confused.

"Go! Hollie! Go!"

But Hollie didn't leave. The men were closing in on us.

"Listen, kid," I heard one of them say, "just give us the coin, okay? Come on now, don't be stupid."

I took my jacket off and threw it to the side as far as I could, hoping Hollie would go over to it.

"There! Hollie! Go there!"

I pointed hard and looked stern. The men were almost on us.

"Go!"

Then I turned and dove into the harbour. The cold was a shock; I knew I couldn't stay long. Swimming underwater for thirty seconds, I surfaced and turned to see if they had followed me. They hadn't. They were standing on the edge of the pier, and they were holding Hollie!

"Let him go!" I yelled. "Let him go!"

I was so angry.

"Give us the coin!" they yelled.

"I don't have it!"

"Give us the coin," said the man with Hollie, "or else . . ."

He raised his fist over Hollie's head in a threatening way. Now I was truly scared.

"Okay! Okay! Don't hurt him! I'll give it to you! Don't hurt him!"

I swam over to a ladder on the pier. The two men leaned over the edge together, one of them still holding onto Hollie. I climbed halfway up.

"Put my dog down and then I'll give you the coin," I said.

"Give us the coin *first*, then I'll put the dog down."

I didn't trust him. If I gave him the coin he'd probably hold onto Hollie to get more. And then, Hollie did something amazing. He squirmed out of the man's arms, ran about fifteen feet away and peered down at me, whining.

"You can do it, Hollie!" I said.

Before the man could grab him again, Hollie leapt from the pier. It was only a ten foot drop but that was a lot for a small dog. I jumped off the ladder and swam over to him.

"Way to go, Hollie! Way to go!"

I looked up at the two men and saw that they had turned around and were talking to someone. They pointed to me. A policeman appeared.

"Are you all right?" he said.

I nodded. The policeman bent down over the top of the ladder and gestured for me to come up.

"You'd better come out of the water son; it's too cold to be swimming," he said.

I swam over with Hollie and held onto him as I climbed the ladder. At the top, the policeman helped us up.

"These two men said that your dog fell in. Is that true? Hey! Where did they go?"

He jumped to his feet and looked around the dock.

"What's going on here? Why would those men leave?"

I didn't know what to say. I didn't want to tell him who I was and why the men were chasing me.

"Ummm. I don't know. I guess they saw me jump in after my dog. But I don't think they could swim."

The policeman eyed me closely.

"Well. You had better get out of those wet clothes. I'll take you home. Where do you live?"

"Ummm, actually I was supposed to meet my family at a pizzeria."

"Which pizzeria?"

"Piero's."

"Okay, I'll take you there. Come with me to the car."

He wasn't asking, he was telling. I followed him to his police car. He opened the back door and Hollie and I climbed in. Then he shut it. I didn't like that because the door automatically locked and we couldn't get out until he let us out. He climbed into the front and got on his radio and told the base he was giving me a lift to meet my parents. Then he said something about the two men and used a couple of code numbers. I reached into my pocket to check if the coin was still there. Happily, it was.

John, Jenny, Becky and Ricky stared out the window of the pizzeria as we pulled up in the police car. The policeman got out first and opened the door for us. John came out to greet us.

"Is this your son?" said the policeman.

"Yes," said John, not missing a beat. "What happened?"

From the window I could see Jenny's worried face.

"Well, it seems his dog fell off the dock and he went in after him. That's what he says. Can you think of any reason why a couple of men might be chasing him?"

"Chasing him? Heavens, no!"

John looked at me and smiled. "Was anybody chasing you, Alfred?"

"I don't think so," I said, trying to sound innocent.

The policeman looked at me. "Listen now, you stay away from the dock with your little doggie there, okay? You shouldn't go so close to the water by yourself anyway, you understand?"

"Yes, officer. I understand."

"Thanks for bringing him to us," said John.

"You have yourselves a good day now," said the police-man. "Enjoy your pizza."

"Thank you, officer," we said.

In the pizzeria I had to explain everything, much to Jenny's horror. I saw her exchange worried looks with John. She started to hint that maybe I was too young to be all alone; that it was too dangerous. Fortunately, I could see from John's expression that he understood me, that I had made my life's choice, come what may.

"I know you will be a whole lot more careful now, Alfred," he said, trying to reassure her.

"You bet I will." I meant it.

After a week, I was anxious to return to the sub. The sea was beckoning. As interesting as the city was, it was no match for the adventure of a sailor's life. Besides, winter was on its way — sooner to Newfoundland than anywhere else — and I didn't want to get caught in the ice, not to mention how anxious I was to see Ziegfried again and show him the crew and the treasure. Jenny tearfully asked me to stay; even suggesting I live with them permanently and return to school. I thought that was a terrible idea, but John saved me by telling her I was already a man, no longer a boy. What I was learning, he said, no school could teach.

We fitted the fridge-freezer and microwave into the sub

and stocked them with pies, frozen pizzas and cookies. We took turns filming ourselves in the house and in the sub. Then, in the middle of night, with a snowstorm in the forecast, I gathered Hollie and Seaweed and we went to sea.

Chapter Twenty-six

S able Island stretched out in front of us, flat and white and nearly invisible in the blowing snow. I opened the hatch to test the wind, then sailed to the sheltered side, where the waves were smaller. I motored as close as possible — just a couple of hundred feet or so — and dropped anchor. Donning my new sea-parka, with pockets large enough for the video camera on one side and Hollie on the other, I inflated the dinghy, sealed the hatch and paddled towards shore. Seaweed stayed on the bow.

Gently we bumped the beach and I jumped out, pulling the dinghy up behind us. It was snowing so hard I doubted

we'd see anything at all, but I had to try. I wanted to film the island's famous ponies for Ziegfried, for Christmas.

Tying the dinghy to a log, we went up the beach. After fifteen minutes we had seen nothing but my tracks in the snow, and the storm showed no sign of weakening.

"What should we do, Hollie? Go further, or go back?"

I look down at his eager little face, blinking through heavy snowflakes. He looked happy enough.

"Okay, we'll go a little further."

Fifteen minutes later we still hadn't seen anything but my footsteps, so I stopped and turned around. I had taken only a few steps when I heard something, or, rather, felt it through the ground. The ponies! I pulled out the video camera and got ready. The ponies came closer and closer, until I was afraid they would run right over us.

"Hey!" I shouted. "Hey!"

But they didn't stop. I bent down and braced myself. They came so close, with a loud punching of their hooves in the snow, but we never saw them.

We returned to the beach, but the dinghy was gone! Neither could we see the submarine.

Don't worry, I thought, we must simply have walked crookedly back to the beach. I turned and walked along the water for ten minutes, but found nothing. So, I turned and walked twenty minutes in the opposite direction. Nothing. Now I was worried. The sub had been sitting for an hour and a half. Even with only a small current it might have

drifted. But where was the dinghy?

For a whole hour I raced back and forth along the beach, getting more and more upset. Suddenly, I stopped.

"*Solve* the problem! Don't just whine about it."

The word, "whine," made me think of Hollie, and that gave me an idea. I opened the pocket and put him down in the snow.

"Go find the dinghy, Hollie! Go find it!"

He looked up with his intelligent little face, so eager to please, and took off. I ran after him. The snow was so deep he had to jump in and out of it like a rabbit, but he went straight in one direction until he reached a mound of sand, covered in snow. I sighed and shrugged my shoulders.

"No, Hollie, that's just a mound of sand."

Hollie let out a sharp and insistent bark.

"It's just sand," I said.

But he wouldn't give up.

"Look!" I said, and gave the mound a kick.

My kick dislodged a pile of snow and revealed the bright orange skin of the dinghy.

"Oh! Hollie! You found it! What a smart dog you are!"

I pulled the dinghy down to the water, paddled out and found the sub not far from where we had left it. Sitting on the hatch and looking very unimpressed with the weather, was the other member of the crew. The three of us climbed inside and sealed the hatch. I hung up the parka and put on a pot of tea. The famous ponies would just have to wait for another season. We would be back.

While the tea was steeping, I deflated the dinghy and put a pizza in the microwave. Hollie and Seaweed jumped up and down with anticipation. You never ate alone in this submarine.

We pulled anchor and went out to where we could dive to a hundred feet and catch some sleep. I must have been very tired, because I slept a long time, and was only wakened by a tugging at my feet. The crew was restless. It was one of those sleeps where you wake up not knowing where you are. It took me a while to get my bearings, even to remember where we had submerged for the day. Coming to the surface I discovered it was already day again! Had I slept twenty-four hours? Even stranger was that Sable Island was nowhere in sight. Was it possible we had drifted in a current? Well, no matter, I thought, there was no damage done.

I was about to start the engine and head northeast, towards Cape Breton and Newfoundland, when the radar beeped. There was a vessel ten miles west of us. A moment later there were two beeps, and then three. That was a little unusual, I thought, three ships travelling together. I had my finger on the engine switch when the three beeps became four, and then five. The ships were not moving very fast, but were coming towards us and seemed to be weaving around each other, as if they were changing places. What on earth were they doing? I climbed the portal to look. The storm was over and the sky was clear. From where we were, the ships appeared to be freighters of different sizes. They closed

the distance between us to five miles and I wondered if I ought to run or dive and hide. Then I noticed that a space began to grow between one of the ships and the other four. Submerging to periscope level, I felt like a WWI sub waiting for its prey. Little did I suspect the danger in which we were lying.

At three miles I could see that the ship closest to us was an old freighter. It appeared to have cut its engines and was drifting. I couldn't see anyone on board. The other ships were a mile on the far side of it and had stopped also. Then I felt a concussive vibration. What on earth was that? Surfacing, I climbed out and scanned the old freighter with binoculars. There was no sign of activity, but I could tell it was a really old ship and not what you would call seaworthy. And then it occurred to me — was it deserted? A few seconds later I saw something fall out of the air and strike the deck of the ship. There was a flash of fire, and then . . . a powerful explosion that roared through my ears and shook the sub. Still, I didn't understand. What was happening?

Nobody appeared on deck to put out the fire. A second thing dropped out of the sky. But this time I saw it clearly. It was a missile! The ship was being fired upon!

My first thoughts were that people would be jumping overboard and that maybe I should try to save them. But no one appeared. The fire was growing on the ship. Suddenly another missile appeared. It passed narrowly by the bow, landed in the water and exploded. The explosion knocked

the sub's lights out for a second and made a loud bang. Hollie started to whine. I wanted to get out of there, but hesitated in case there were people fleeing the ship. I scanned the ship again but saw no one, not a single sign of life. I turned the binoculars towards the other ships and . . . suddenly I understood.

It was the navy! They were target practising! They were going to blow up the abandoned freighter and sink it. And we were in their target area!

There were a few more explosions, and then, the strangest sound, which I assumed to be the old freighter sinking. I felt a mix of fear and sadness: sadness for the old ship going to a watery grave, fear that the navy would see us and chase us.

They did! One of the ships left the group and came immediately towards us. And she was fast! There was no way to outrun her. As the sonar showed the navy ship closing in, I knew I had to make a decision: either surface and risk losing the sub, or try to hide. But we couldn't hide anywhere near the surface; their radar could easily spot us. Underwater their sonar would certainly pick up the whir of the propeller under battery power, even the shape of the sub if they were close enough. And then, if they wanted to drop depth charges — exploding devices that would damage the sub — they could force us to surface, or, worse, sink us.

They were closing in; I had to decide. If they took the sub, my exploring days would be over, at least for several more years. That decided it for me. I shut off the sonar, dove

to three hundred feet, the deepest I dared, turned ninety degrees towards Nova Scotia, climbed up on the bike and started pedalling.

Maybe I was crazy. I didn't know what else to do. For the next half-hour I braced myself for an explosion. But it never came. Because I couldn't turn on the sonar without letting them know exactly where we were, I couldn't know where *they* were. If they did have us on sonar, which they probably did, they would know by our size and shape we were the same sub who had assisted the coastguard recently. Surely they wouldn't sink a friendly sub?

Five hours later I was still pedalling. The coast was at least another ten hours away. I decided to rise to periscope level and take a peek. It was dark now. On the horizon, to the east, I saw the lights of a ship. Diving to a hundred feet, I shared a snack with the crew and resumed pedalling. Five hours later I rose to periscope level again. The horizon was clear. We were only an hour from shore by engine. Was it worth the risk? I surfaced and mulled over it for awhile. I was about to flip the engine switch, when I had a second thought. Most of the bad decisions I had made could have been prevented with a little caution. I climbed the portal, opened the hatch and took a good look around. There was nothing but darkness and a moon behind clouds. But as I leaned against the portal and watched the moon come free of the clouds, I saw it reflect off something on the horizon. I strained to make out what it was. Then it turned sideways

and I saw its silhouette clearly. It was a ship, with its lights out! It must have been following us in, assuming quite correctly that we would take the shortest route to land. Perhaps on bicycle power they had not been able to detect us. Or perhaps they had identified us and did not want to risk sinking us. Likely they were hoping we would surface and they'd spot us. Whew! That was close. Diving once again, I continued pedalling, and pedalled all the way in. The navy must have concluded we were not a threat and were no longer worth following. I found a secluded cove, let Seaweed out, dove to seventy-five feet and went to bed completely exhausted.

Chapter Twenty-seven

Catching a glimpse of land around Port aux Basques filled me with an unexpected feeling: that I was actually *from* somewhere. Seaweed was a Newfoundland seagull and I was a Newfoundland sailor, and even though I intended to travel all around the world, Newfoundland would always be my home. And Hollie, well, strictly speaking, I *did* find him on the sea, so I suppose he was, in truth, a sea dog.

Most days now it snowed, and it had grown *much* colder. Cold on the sea was a lot colder than on the land. But I did not expect to run into icebergs, which we might have if we returned the way we had come. The west coast of New-

foundland was rugged, beautiful, and less populated, so I assumed we would not run into many people either, or be recognized. Boy, was that wrong!

Our first encounter took place around the tip of Cape Anguille. We were cruising along on the surface in the middle of morning, admiring the snow-covered mountains and looking for a cove to settle for the day. We had the hatch open and I was running down from time to time to check the radar and sonar. At one point we came upon a hidden cove. I was watching the sonar for a suitable spot and turned into the cove without bothering to check with the periscope. I just assumed the cove was uninhabited. It wasn't. Down at the water was a bunch of people gathered at a wedding! We sailed into the little cove right in the middle of the ceremony! By the time I climbed the portal to take a look, I was facing about twenty-five people staring at us as if we had just come from the moon!

They were surprised but very friendly, and insisted we join their reception. I didn't see how we could refuse. So I moored to the dock, sealed the hatch, carried Hollie over and joined the party. It turned out to be a lot of fun. Everyone took pictures of Hollie and Seaweed with the bride and groom, and they said it was the best kind of luck that we had shown up on their wedding day. We ate so much we stumbled back to the sub and slept like logs. A few days later we were on the front of the newspaper again. The picture showed the bride giving Hollie a kiss and Seaweed

standing behind the groom's head. The headline read:

SUBMARINE OUTLAW CRASHES WEDDING! HEADING NORTH!

After that, everyone knew where we were going.

Our second encounter was very different. I had become altogether too relaxed about our visibility. The coastguard didn't seem to be anywhere on the west coast, and the only sea traffic we had encountered so far had been from small boaters. What I neglected to consider were the people with telescopes and short-wave radios. Not only were they able to communicate where we actually were, they could predict where we would be, and when. So much for stealth!

We were crossing the mouth of Bonne Bay in the early hours of morning. As usual, I was seeking a sheltered cove for the day. As we approached Lobster Cove, I heard the radar beep and saw a fishing boat heading out. No matter, I thought, and continued on our way. I planned to wave as we passed. Suddenly another boat came out, and then another. The three boats formed an arc and stopped in front of us. I slowed down. Were they hoping to meet us? I was tired and just wanted to sleep. Then the radar showed two more boats coming from shore behind us, and I got a funny feeling in my stomach. Were they trying to surround us?

As we neared the boats in the front, they narrowed the spaces between and I slowed down even more. The boats behind us came on quickly. I was confused; why would they want to surround us? The water was plenty deep; we could

easily go beneath them and escape. I climbed the portal to take a look and was shocked to see them drop their nets. They were trying to catch us!

The fishing boats formed a semi-circle and tied their nets together, leaving only the side to the beach open. I stopped the sub, otherwise I would have run into them. The water was about seventy-five feet deep; their nets could easily be sitting on the bottom. I didn't know what to do. Was this just a kind of joke? Surely they did not want to damage their nets?

I motored a little closer to shore. The boats closed in on us and the circle grew tighter. Yup, they meant business. Okay, I thought, I am not going to surrender the sub, and I am not responsible for any damage to their nets or boats. Submerging to sixty feet, I watched on the sonar as they closed the circle even tighter. I tried to imagine the wall of netting surrounding us, and then I got an idea. Turning the batteries to full power, I began to spin the sub in a circle, like a spinning top. Around and around we went, without actually changing our position. I was hoping to create a whirlpool, which would lift the nets off the seafloor far enough for us to slip underneath. The only problem was that I couldn't know if it was working; I could only hope it was. Around and around we spun. It must have created quite a rotational force in the water. After five minutes of spinning I straightened out and headed directly towards the net. I felt for any tugging on the sub as we passed through the barricade. Nothing. Hah! We were free! A quarter of a

mile out I surfaced and climbed the portal. The circle of boats had broken and they turned seaward as soon as they saw the sub. I submerged again and that was the last they ever saw of us.

After that, I didn't take any more chances. I went back to my habit of choosing sleeping spots *before* the sun was up. I also avoided contact with the few boats we happened to run by. We had just one more encounter, but it was a good one.

We were passing the point at Port au Choix. It was twilight and foggy enough to hide us from shore. So I surfaced and was about to crank the engine to full speed. I just climbed the portal for a breath of fresh air first. The radar was clear but visibility was low. Out of the corner of my eye I thought I saw something on the water. Now I saw it, and now I didn't. In my experience, that usually meant there *was* something. Slowly, I steered towards the area. Sure enough, there was a dory tossing on the water. In it this time was not a dog but a boy!

He was twelve, just two years younger than I but looked a lot younger, I thought. It was growing dark and he was a mile offshore in a dory with nothing but two oars and a bottle of water. When he saw the sub he cried out, "Hey! Hey!"

"Hello!" I called back. "What are you doing out here? Are you crazy?"

"I just wanted to meet you," he said.

"How long have you been out here?"

"All day."

"All day!"

I couldn't believe it. He must have been freezing and dead tired. I felt sorry for him.

"You'd better come in and warm up," I said.

"Can I?"

I nodded and steered over to the dory.

"Throw me your rope and I'll tie up your boat."

His name was Daniel. It turned out he was growing up in a small fishing village, but, like me, didn't want to become a fisherman. He said that ever since he first saw the sub on TV he had decided that's what he wanted to do — build a submarine and go to sea. He was keeping a scrapbook of newspaper clippings of sightings of us. That's how he knew we'd be passing by. He had been coming out in his dory every day for a week! When he told me that, I knew he was serious.

Daniel was shivering when he followed me inside. Hollie was delighted to have company and came right up to him and wagged his little tail. Seaweed couldn't have cared less.

"Don't mind him," I said. "Seagulls are only friendly when you have food in your hand."

Daniel stared all around as if he were in a treasure room. I could understand. I remembered how excited I was when we first started putting wood in the interior.

"Don't you realize how dangerous it is to be out in a dory, alone and far from shore? What if you were swept away in a current?"

He didn't answer. He just petted Hollie, who looked up at

me to see if it was okay. I realized I must have sounded dis-
approving. Enough of that.

"Do you want some pizza?"

His face brightened.

"You have pizza here?"

"You bet! You have to be comfortable when you go to sea."

He smiled.

"It's nice and warm in here."

"Here. I'll show you how things work."

I showed Daniel the control-panel and explained the
switches and how the systems worked. I took him aft to see
the engine and batteries. Then we sat and had pizza and tea.
He was starving.

"I can't believe you have a bicycle in here."

"Sometimes it's the only way to get around."

"Is that how you sneaked away from the coastguard?"

"Yup. That's how I escaped from a lot of things. But it's
really slow."

"Can I look out the periscope?"

"Sure. But it's foggy; you won't see much. Why don't we
go closer to shore; you'll see better."

So we started the engine and motored in and took turns
peering at the lights on shore. Then we untied his dory and
I showed him how to submerge and how to watch the sonar.
He was like a kid on Christmas. But I wondered if his parents would be worrying about him.

"Won't they think you are lost at sea?"

"No. They don't know where I am."

"They don't even know you are out on the water? All week? Don't they care?"

"Not really."

"They must care *some*?"

He stared at the floor.

"What about your teachers at school?"

"They prefer it when I'm not there, 'cause I get into so much trouble."

After a few hours I took Daniel home. We sailed right into his cove in the fog and docked at the pier. I didn't think anyone would see us. I promised I would write to him.

"You *promise*?" he said as he climbed onto the pier.

"I promise."

He waved as we pulled away.

"Thanks for the ride!" he shouted.

"You're welcome! Remember: the sea doesn't care if you are sincere!"

As I watched Daniel disappear, I couldn't help thinking how far I had come in two and a half years, and how grateful I was to Ziegfried for that journey.

Chapter Twenty-eight

It was a surprise to me that the most exciting part of my first voyage was the coming home. I wouldn't have expected that. Nothing, not even finding the treasure, was as exciting as the thought of seeing Ziegfried again and introducing him to Hollie and Seaweed.

But coming home was not easy. A storm caught us off guard as we sailed up the Strait of Belle Isle. Once in awhile I caught a glimpse of a light on shore; otherwise, sailing around the point of the peninsula was like riding around the moon. We had to submerge often to get out of rough sailing, and more than once took shelter in a tiny cove, running the

engine for hours to recharge the batteries. Once we did round the point and pass St. Anthony, the storm abated. But there were almost no lights on shore now because there were no people. The last stretch of our trip — down the east side of the Northern Peninsula — was the least populated.

We listened to the radio a lot and danced and sang. Hollie was a terrific dancer, and his singing was no worse than mine. Seaweed was a passable dancer — not too exciting — he just hopped from one foot to the other. But his singing was really awful, so we didn't encourage him too much.

We also listened to talk shows. My favourite was a call-in show where people expressed their opinions on current issues. One day the topic was, "Should homeowners be allowed to hang clotheslines in new urban residential areas?"

That was pretty boring, but people became really worked up over it. It was a good thing they weren't all in the same room or they'd be fighting for sure.

The next day the topic was better, "Should dogs and cats be allowed to get married?"

I don't know what Hollie thought about that, but the people who called in had very strong opinions. I wondered what Sheba would think.

The topic on the third day really caught my attention:

"Should the coastguard make more of an effort to catch the Submarine Outlaw?"

When I heard that I stopped pedalling and sat down by the radio and listened.

The first caller said that the coastguard should leave me alone; that everybody had a right to do what they wanted on the sea. Nobody owns the sea, he said. I liked that answer.

The second caller disagreed. They should capture me, she said, and have a trial and decide whether or not I had done anything wrong. Yikes! I wouldn't want *her* to be on the jury.

The next caller said they should definitely catch me and make an example of me; otherwise, who knows what is lurking beneath the waters of our harbours? And, if the coastguard can't catch one little submarine, what good are they? It doesn't make a body feel protected, she said.

I really liked the next one. He said that the coastguard should pay me for keeping an eye out for strangers in our waters. I could be like an underwater deputy.

Then someone called in claiming to be with the coastguard. He said the coastguard didn't catch me simply because they didn't want to put me in danger by chasing me, but that they would appreciate it if I would voluntarily report my vessel at any local harbour. Hmmm, I thought. No thanks.

We were crossing the mouth of White Bay when we hit a block of ice. We struck it on the starboard side and bounced off without damaging the sub, but it knocked me right off the bike.

Okay, I thought, I'll be more careful. Then, we hit another one. It was a smaller chunk but we hit it dead on. When the sub collided, I could hear the wooden beams creak. Now I

better understood Ziegfried's ingenious design — the wood supported the steel by absorbing the shock, so the sub "bounced" like a wooden ball, instead of receiving a dent, or worse, a puncture. Ziegfried had also placed heavy-duty rubber wedges between the wood and metal to soften the blow. All the same, I was determined to avoid another collision. For the very last leg to Dark Cove, we rode safely at a hundred feet, under battery power. That was a good idea anyway, so no one in the immediate area could detect us by telescope, or anything else, and know where the "Outlaw Submarine" was docked for the winter.

That was a good question — where *would* we dock for the winter? It occurred to me, we had never made definite plans. I just assumed we would moor the sub around the corner from where we had launched it. In truth, we had never really decided. I realized now, I should have given it more careful thought. As it turned out, Ziegfried had.

We approached Dark Cove at night. I saw the lights of the village and swelled with joy. The feeling of having had a successful voyage was exhilarating. But up on the hill, in the direction of the junkyard, I saw a blinking light. It seemed to be blinking with a pattern. I immediately thought of Morse code. Grabbing my code book, I watched the repeating pattern and wrote down the letters:

"...t h i r t e e n m i l e s w e s t A l f r e d t h i r t e e n m i l e s w e s t A l f r e d t h i r t e e n m i l e s..."

I blinked back with one floodlight:

"O k a y C o p y?"

But there was no response. Likely the light was blinking automatically. Ziegfried was not there.

He wanted to meet me thirteen miles west. I wondered why. Well, he must have had a good reason. I hoped everything was okay in the village. Maybe people had figured everything out. Maybe there were people with cameras there. Maybe the coastguard was there. Or the police! Now I was worried. I hoped Ziegfried hadn't gotten into any trouble.

The shore west of Dark Cove was unpopulated and there wasn't a single light until we reached the thirteen-mile point. Then, I saw one lonely light down by the water. It wasn't easy to see because the shore was a beehive of nooks and crannies and narrow fissures into the rock. Sailing closer, I had to keep an eye on the sonar to stay clear of jutting rocks here and there. It was the last place anyone would want to moor a boat. It was only when we were very close to shore that I realized the light was coming from some sort of boathouse built right onto the rock. It was well hidden from the sea. Through the periscope I saw Ziegfried's hulking silhouette against the boathouse. How on earth, I wondered, had he ever found such a place?

Well, it turned out, he hadn't found it; he had *built* it. Now I learned why I had not been able to reach him all this time — he had been busy building a winter home for the sub.

At periscope depth we glided gently between the jagged rock until we reached the end. Then, slowly, we surfaced.

I kept a lookout through the periscope, to make sure we didn't come up beneath anything. It was a narrow enclosure. I saw Ziegfried standing on a wooden platform next to us. Then, I felt him land heavily on the bow. He opened the hatch.

"Anybody in there?"

"You bet!"

I climbed up and received one of Ziegfried's great bear hugs, which is what I imagined a bear would really feel like. He stared at me for almost a minute and his eyes were watery with excitement and emotion.

"Well, didn't *you* have an adventure? And come back all famous and everything. Boy, have we got a lot to talk about!"

"We sure do. But . . . where did this place come from?"

I looked all around. The boathouse was plain but cozy. In one corner was an old wood stove I recognized from the junkyard. Against one wall was a row of firewood. There were just two windows, and they both faced the sea. The frame was resting on thick wooden beams that had been cut right into the rock.

"I built it," said Ziegfried, proudly. "I bought the land for next to nothing and told people I was building myself a cottage. You know how I don't particularly like to work with wood?"

"I know!"

"Well, this time I actually enjoyed it. I had a heck of a time out here. Wait till you see the upstairs!"

"There's an upstairs?"

"Come and see."

"Wait! I want you to meet the crew."

"Oh *yah,* the seagull."

"Not only."

I went down and got Hollie and carried him out. Ziegfried took one look at him and his face went soft. It was funny to see the heart of such a strong man melt so easily. I handed Hollie over to Ziegfried, and Hollie licked his chin.

"Well, this little fella and me are going to become good friends."

Then Seaweed appeared.

"Hah! Now don't tell me he climbs the ladder himself?"

"All the time."

"Well . . . I just don't know what to say. Come upstairs and have a look."

I followed Ziegfried up the stairs into a small, one-room loft. There was another wood stove, a fridge, table, desk and chair. In one corner was a sleeping cot. There was a bay window with a great view of the sea.

"Wow!" I said. "It is amazing! It is the nicest boathouse anyone ever built. I just love it."

"Well, I'm glad you do, Al, because this is going to be *your* place when you're not at sea."

"Really? You mean, you built it for *me*?"

I didn't know what to say. Then I thought of something else.

"Well . . . I've got something for *you*!"

"For me?"

"Something really special. But you have to come into the sub to see it; it's too heavy for me to carry out by myself."

He frowned the way he did when he was trying to figure something out.

"Something for *me*?" he said, confused.

"Well, actually, we get to share it — fifty-fifty."

"I can't imagine what it is," he said as he followed me back downstairs and into the sub.

"This place looks familiar," he said, crouching down.

I showed him the chest. His mouth dropped.

"Was there anything inside?"

"Yup!"

I lifted the lid and showed him the cutlery. He whistled.

"Wow! Look at that!"

Then I picked up the small chest and handed it to him.

"This was underneath that!"

Ziegfried opened the small chest and burst into a beaming smile.

"Oh my stars, will you look at that? Al, you found a real treasure!"

"Fifty-fifty!" I said. "Like real treasure hunters."

"Oh no, Al. You found it; it's all yours."

I took hold of Ziegfried's arm and looked right into his eyes. This was very important to me.

"If you won't share it with me, half and half, I will sail out tonight and dump it all in the ocean!"

And I meant it.

He took a long stare at me and could see that I really did mean it.

"Well, that would be kind of a waste now, wouldn't it? Okay. Fifty-fifty."

We both burst out laughing. No amount of money could ever have touched the joy I felt then.

Chapter Twenty-nine

I n December, we hoisted the sub out of the water and hung it in the air with cables. Storms lashed the roof of the boathouse and ocean ice creaked and whined like demons outside, but we kept the wood stove roaring and the radio blaring. It was cozy inside the boathouse. Hollie, Seaweed, and I stayed there full-time, sleeping upstairs in the loft. We were inside most of the time, except for our daily walk, when Seaweed took to the air to stretch his wings and Hollie ran around chasing invisible rabbits. But living in the boathouse was a little like living outdoors. Because the ocean did not freeze indoors, Seaweed could paddle in the

open water below, and the wooden boardwalk around the sub allowed Hollie to run round and round. This led to a few interesting encounters when curious seals swam inside, poked their heads up and barked at the little dog and sea-gull looking down at them.

It was Ziegfried's intention to make the sub faster and further ranging. Myself, I was happy with it just the way it was.

"Really, Al," he said, "you want to be as fast as you possibly can. There's no telling what you'll run into when you leave our waters. Look at this."

He held up a magazine with a picture of a rifle.

"What's that?"

"The Kalashnikov assault rifle, or, Ak-47. Says here it is ". . . reliable, easily cleaned, cheap and deadly, making it the weapon of choice for Third World armies, terrorists, and . . . pirates."

"Pirates?"

"You'd better believe it. You cannot imagine how happy pirates were to get their hands on machine guns, speedboats and radar. Stealth is great, Al, for sure, but even pirates could figure out how to use sophisticated sonar. I want to know that you could outrun them if you ever met up with them."

To this end, he fashioned a dolphin nose and welded it to the front of the sub.

"Don't laugh, Al, nature is master designer. Dolphins are the fastest things in the water."

I had to smile when the nose was attached. If you drew a couple of eyes on either side, the front of the sub would look just like a dolphin. I wondered what the real dolphins were going to think.

Other modifications he had planned included replacing the old Beetle motor with a turbo-charged diesel engine which would be more fuel efficient, powerful and noisy; exchanging the propeller for one with more aggressive torque; adding another fuel tank; and doubling the number of batteries so that the sub could run twenty hours submerged. He also wanted to add more bicycle gears, since, in three years, I had doubled my pedalling strength. He even had visions of inserting the propulsion systems of two second-hand jet-skies into the stern of the sub on either side of the propeller so as to add a powerful burst of speed for emergencies. That gave me visions of the sub plowing through the water like a rocket. In fact, by "burst of speed," Ziegfried meant about five knots per hour faster.

But all of these modifications would take time and work, and that left no question as to how the winter would be spent. I only hoped that, come the summer, when the crew was restless and the sea beckoning for another voyage, the sub would be ready to sail.

On Christmas Eve, in the early morning, we climbed into the truck and drove to Grand Falls. Hollie sat in the front and Seaweed rode on top. In Grand Falls, we parked the

truck at the bus station and went inside to look for some-one. We found him curled up on the floor, asleep, his head on his jacket.

"Is this him?" asked Ziegfried.

"Yup."

"He looks so young."

"He's the same age I was when we started building the sub. How did you know then that I'd be worth all the trouble?"

"Easy. You were the only person ever brave enough to sneak into my yard. I figured you'd be brave enough to go to sea in a submarine."

He reached down and tugged at Daniel's collar. Daniel woke with a fearful look — it being the first time he had ever set eyes upon Ziegfried.

"Quick," I said, "grab your stuff. We've got a long ways to go before dark."

"Are we really going to see the Queen of Sheba?" asked Daniel in a sleepy voice.

"Sort of."

We had left Ziegfried's birds in the care of my grand-mother and grandfather. Ziegfried had been right. Once they learned that the submarine was not just a fanciful dream they were able to accept my decision not to become a fisherman. My grandfather even asked me questions about being at sea, which was the biggest compliment he could ever have given me.

It was twilight by the time we reached Sheba's island. Bundled up in parkas, hats and mitts, we steered through choppy water in a small outboard motorboat while a light snow fell all around us. The sun had gone down and the night looked foreboding, but we were merry with Christmas spirit. Still, the closer we came to Sheba's, the more nervous Ziegfried became. He even suggested just dropping us off and picking us up.

"But if you don't come, she'll be terribly disappointed. She said she would throw herself at the mermaids if we didn't come for Christmas. She really said that."

"Well, I suppose we don't want that to happen."

When we came around the last island we saw the glow of Christmas lights. Sheba had strung rows of lights all around her little cove. As we entered the cove we saw her emerge with her grand array of animals. She was wearing a red and green dress and was glittering with jewelry. Her hair was flaming red and dancing with sparkles. I could see that Ziegfried and Daniel were as bewitched as I had first been.

"Welcome! Oh, welcome!" Sheba cried, with a song-like voice. "Oh, Alfred! You have come back, just as you promised!"

She came down and hugged me as I stepped from the boat. Then she saw Hollie in my pocket and exclaimed, "Oooooohhhh! Such a treasure!"

I introduced Daniel. She bent down and looked deeply into his eyes and took hold of his hands. She must have

really looked like a queen to him. Then Ziegfried stepped from the boat. I had never seen him looking so uncomfortable, but Sheba offered him her hand and he took it with tremendous care. Their eyes met and she spoke to him, but Ziegfried could not get a word out, even though he tried.

"Come, friends! Come into our home and be happy!" said Sheba.

We followed her up the path, while the dogs crowded around us.

We stayed for three days. It was absolutely wonderful. While Daniel and I followed Sheba around and helped her prepare meals and fabulous desserts, Ziegfried set about making every possible repair. As soon as he finished one, he searched for another. I told him to relax, that Sheba's cottage would not fall apart without another repair, but he wouldn't listen. I saw Sheba steal quick glances at him as he moved gigantically about her cottage. The dogs and cats climbed all over him while he made his repairs, but he never flinched. He worked as if their presence was a necessary part of the job. In Sheba's world, it was.

When it was time to go, we were all feeling a little bigger around our bellies. Ziegfried said there were important repairs to make to the foundation of Sheba's cottage, and they had discussed his returning to make them. I don't think Ziegfried had spoken more than a handful of words to Sheba directly but now it seemed to be his mission in life to return as soon as possible. Her final words to him were, "I will keep the stove warm." And her eyes twinkled.

On the way home, Ziegfried was silent. I couldn't get more than one-word answers out of him. Daniel was also quiet. When he did speak, he showed that he was thinking deeply about something.

"Do you think," he said, breaking the silence in the truck, "do you think that maybe there are places on earth that nobody has ever seen?"

I smiled. It seemed like a pretty good question to me.

Our next stop was my grandparents' house. My grandmother had prepared a traditional fisherman's Christmas feast for us, which included fish chowder, baked fish and fish pie. It was delicious too. My grandparents didn't talk a whole lot but I could tell that they were glad we had come. My grandfather even surprised me by taking an interest in Daniel. Halfway though our supper he suddenly turned to him, "So . . . Daniel, you're gonna be a fisherman, are you?"

The question caught Daniel by surprise.

"Huh? Oh, . . . no. No, I'm gonna be an explorer."

"An *explorer*?"

"Yah."

My grandfather stared at the floor for awhile. Then he raised his head and took a deep breath.

"Well," he said, "I suppose we could always use some more of those."

ABOUT THE AUTHOR

 Philip Francis Roy was born and raised in Antigonish, Nova Scotia. He grew up beside the ocean, and it now features in many of the stories he writes. His university studies included music and history, but he also knew from an early age that he wanted to write novels. *Submarine Outlaw*, his first published novel, is the result of a lifelong fascination with submarines and a secret desire to build one. "If teens enjoy reading *Submarine Outlaw* half as much as I enjoyed writing it," says Philip, "I will feel very rewarded indeed." Philip has many other stories waiting in the docks, including an exciting sequel to *Submarine Outlaw*, coming soon.

Marquis Book Printing Inc.

Québec, Canada
2009

Lawyer
for the
Cat

Available in ebook now and paperback in 2017